Lustlocked

Also by Matt Wallace

The Sin du Jour Series
Envy of Angels

The Failed Cities
The Next Fix (collection)

Slingers (novella series)

LUSTLOCKED

MATT WALLACE

A TOM DOHERTY ASSOCIATES BOOK

NEW YORK

This is a work of fiction. All of the characters, organizations, and
events portrayed in this novella are either products of the author's
imagination or are used fictitiously.

LUSTLOCKED

A Tor.com Book
Published by Tom Doherty Associates, LLC
175 Fifth Avenue
New York, NY 10010

www.tor.com

Tor® is a registered trademark of Tom Doherty Associates, LLC.

ISBN 978-1-4668-9283-5 (e-book)
ISBN 978-0-7653-8778-3 (trade paperback)

First Edition: January 2016

For Nikki, my real-life sin du jour

PART I

ALL PARTIES HEREIN

GONE FISHIN'

They aren't biting today.

Moon sits in a rust-plagued boat bobbing on candy-bright torpedo pontoons the color of caution tape. His line is dropped in the pearl-gray waters of the lake surrounding them. He's currently humming the theme song from the classic science fiction television series *Quantum Leap* for the eleventh time.

As the tune runs out of momentum Moon tries switching to the *Legend of Zelda* theme, but gives up after humming the first bar.

"Are you guys almost done down there?" he asks the impossibly small piece of composite concealed in his right ear. "I'm fuckin' bored."

"Us 'guys' are rigging the final charge now," Cindy's irritated voice answers him over the earpiece.

"Sorry," he says. "*Folks. People.* Whatever. Nonoffensive gender-neutral pronoun. When did you graduate from Feminist Police Academy, Cindy?"

"Words matter."

Ritter's voice, its tone ever even, joins the conversation in Moon's skull: "Wouldn't think you'd need to be told that, Moon."

"How'm I supposed to keep up with every new edition of the politically correct dictionary?"

"I meant more the fact you're someone who narrowly avoids death by rogue magic spell every other week and you're sittin' on your ass questioning the validity of words and their power."

"Oh."

Hara grunts over the four-way communications line.

The three of them are currently floating several dozen yards below the surface of the water. Clad in skintight wet suits and next-generation scuba gear, Ritter, Cindy, and Hara have spent the last hour sinking military-grade depth charges in the unassuming provincial lake.

Cindy, lengths of acrylic plastic chain coiled around the torso of her suit, examines the final mine she's tethered to the lake bed. The nondescript sphere rises higher than the other seven, straining just a few yards from the surface.

"All right, the break is set," Cindy informs them. "My record's a break of six. If this works I'll kick the shit out of that."

"You're an artist," Ritter says.

"Of course, those were incendiary charges," she adds with a touch of regret, ignoring the compliment.

"Frying the thing comes later, Cin. Head on up. Get ready to bring it onto the boat."

"Roger."

Cindy's flipper-footed legs scissor rapidly and fluidly, propelling her up through the murky water.

Ritter and Hara swim to the edges of the blast zone, designated by the buoys with lit bottoms Cindy has arranged for them. They both reach past the lengths of chain wrapped around their own bodies and remove foot-long batons. The push of a button extends each by another two feet, their ends crackling with plasmatic fire.

When Cindy emerges from the depths, Moon is reeling in his sad little fishing line. She pulls herself into the boat with an easy, athletic grace and removes her aspirator, goggles, and hood, dropping them and smoothing her hands over her dark scalp.

"I kinda miss the orange," Moon comments as he watches her shake stray droplets from the natural cloud of her usually cornrowed hair.

"It was auburn and it was a phase," Cindy dryly informs him. "Some kind of *Mad TV,* Debra Wilson nostalgia. I don't know." And then, annoyed suddenly: "What do you care?"

"I dunno." Moon says, shrugging. "Your hair's different from most of the chicks I know."

Cindy sighs. "If only your stereotypical fascination

with black hair was the most offensive thing about you, Moon. If only."

"Hey, you're sure we're safe up here, right?" he asks her.

She begins peeling away the other parts of her diving suit. "I was EOD for four years."

"Yeah, but . . . I mean, that was the navy, right?"

Cindy stops and stares at him blankly.

"What the fuck is that supposed to mean?"

"I . . . nothing. It's just . . . you know."

"Look, I wouldn't question you on how precise your bong hits or Elder fucking Scrolls strategy is, all right?"

"Fair enough."

Over their earpieces, Ritter: "We're in position, Cin. Light it up."

Cindy reaches into a rucksack at the bottom of the boat and removes an iPhone. There's only one icon on its lit screen.

The deepest charge is swaying just above the lake bed, tethered by a scant dozen links of water-resistant chain. Cindy has planted it a few feet from the mouth of a shallow cave created by a pile of jagged rocks that have rested against each other for centuries.

"Ignition in five, four, three, two, one," Cindy counts off, then detonates the bottommost charge.

The sphere at the end of its short leash breaks apart

silently, but the shock wave it disperses topples the rocks shaping the dark maw of the cave. Before they separate and glide to the ground, a large green conical shape launches, panicked, from within.

Its frantic, iridescent tail immediately fans too close to another charge tethered several feet above the one that's just destroyed its lair.

Rather than being blown apart, the creature is blasted several yards off its current course by a harmless but powerful sonic wave. Attempting to escape its force only drives the creature into the next mine, detonating it, and then the next, each one corralling it in a predetermined pattern toward the surface.

Ritter and Hara wait on either side of its slalomlike dash, ready to drive it back onto the correct path with their plasma torches should it deviate too far.

They never get the chance.

Cindy's break is perfect.

When the creature trips the final mine Ritter lowers his baton and removes an underwater remote from the belt of his suit.

"Get ready for immersion," he warns Cindy and Moon over their earpieces.

He presses a single button.

The surface of the lake, meanwhile, has remained calm throughout the sonic chaos below.

That all changes as a twelve-foot diameter of water is abruptly sucked down, creating an instant whirlpool.

Moon's wasn't the only fishing line sunk into the water. A giant mechanical crane arm hovers above the boat, attached to a large flatbed truck parked beside the lake.

A quartet of heavy cables splayed from the tip of the crane arm has been resting beneath the water since before the trio descended its depths.

Now they suddenly draw tight, pulling a large fishing net from the depths of the lake.

The team's quarry, the massive creature of the cave, is caught in its grid.

It's a fish.

It is, however, a very big fish.

The great fish is the size of a toddler. It has the drooping, catfishlike features of a sad old man and fiery, ageless eyes that burn grudgingly at Moon and Cindy through the netting.

"Jesus," Moon says as he watches the net rotate from the crane arm. "That's what goblins eat?"

"Only on very special occasions," Cindy informs him.

A moment later Ritter and Hara emerge from the lake, swimming to the boat's stern.

Ritter, still in the water, removes his aspirator. "Break worked like gangbusters," he shouts up at Cindy.

She tilts her head at Moon triumphantly without saying a word.

In response he makes a jerking motion with his hand above his pelvis.

At which point Cindy leans back and kicks him in the chest, sending him sprawling backward into the bottom of the boat.

"Goddammit, Cindy!" Moon yells through his own doubled-over legs.

The foursome steer the boat back to shore, where Ritter, Cindy, and Hara change out of their diving suits.

Next to their flatbed truck is an old jeep. They load the fish into a customized freshwater tank bolted in the back.

"How the hell are we supposed to clear customs with this thing?" Moon asks.

"We're going to put a wool coat on it and tell them it's your grandpa," Cindy tells him.

Ritter snaps the lid on the tank closed. "Let's go."

Hara doesn't move.

He's the first one to hear the rumbling of the engines.

They all look to the brush surrounding the small lake as a trio of motors breaks through it. Three surplus military vehicles, two jeeps and a half-track, imported from some Eastern Bloc country that no longer exists grind to halt in a uniform row between them and the only road access to the lake.

The men they bear wear the standard paramilitary uniform of camouflaged fatigues decorated with absolutely no insignia of any kind. They belong to one of the half-dozen factions warring for control of the troubled region to which Ritter has brought his team to fish.

The leader of the unit is a scarred-face man in his late twenties so denoted by his swagger and the fact that he's clearly the only adult in the squad. Not a single one of his soldiers is over the age of eighteen, including the lithe, smiling teenager grasping a fifty-caliber machine gun mounted on the half-track and currently pointed at Sin du Jour's stocking and receiving department.

Their captain steps down from one of the jeeps. The rest of the militia unit carry secondhand automatic rifles, while he walks unburdened, with only a pistol holstered at his hip.

He steps away from the pack, his eyes immediately recognizing Ritter as the leader of his own group.

The militia captain smiles.

"White man, white man, come to pluck the fruit of my land," he sing-songs in a thick accent.

"Not white, not a man," Cindy mutters in exasperation.

"Cin," Ritter hisses at her.

To the captain he says, "Is there a problem?"

"You are trespassing," the militia captain informs him.

"This is Benjabi land," Ritter says resolutely. "We negotiated with the tribe for the right to be here."

The captain nods thoughtfully. "This *was* Benjabi land. Now it is mine. Just like the things you give them."

The self-appointed captain slaps a hand against a crate, one among dozens concealed beneath a tarp in the back of their jeep.

Ritter and the rest crane their heads slightly, all of them recognizing the medical supplies and dry food they gave the Benjabi elders in exchange for their permission to fish the lake.

"Oh, so you guys are just total dicks, huh?"

"Shut up, Moon," Ritter commands.

Atop the half-track, the squad's heavy gunner cycles the fifty-caliber behemoth's action pointedly.

Hara slowly but deliberately moves to step between Moon and the weapon.

Ritter extends an arm to halt him, the rest of his body remaining perfectly still.

"What do you want?" he asks the captain.

"Everything."

Ritter nods. He looks to Cindy briefly, whose hands seem to visibly ache for want of a weapon, then back at the squad's leader.

"Fuck you."

His smile never falters.

"Kill the little one first," their leader instructs his gunner.

The post-pubescent wrapped around the fifty-caliber machine gun opens fire.

At first it seems as if Moon is screaming in agony while bullets shred the meat of his body, but two things quickly become apparent to everyone gathered beside the lake.

It isn't bullets splattering Moon.

And the screams aren't his.

When the heavy-caliber automatic gunfire ceases the body that falls is that of the militia soldier. He creates a loud and deep metallic clanging sound when he hits the top of the half-track.

Most of his exposed flesh is now battered lead, the seams of it horrifically fused to the parts of him that are still covered by human skin.

Moon, very much alive and unharmed, begins wiping dark gore from himself in thick sheets.

"Dude, this is fucking disgusting! Seriously! Not cool!"

The other soldiers begin murmuring in abject terror. Most of them saw the metal overtake their comrade's flesh like a mystic industrial plague as he fired the fifty-cal. The rest watched as blood and biological waste rather than fire and lead spat from the weapon's barrel.

Many of them are saying prayers.

The others are speaking in their own language of witches and demons.

No one is certain who breaks first, but in the next moment they all drop their weapons and run, abandoning the vehicles altogether.

All but their leader.

"What in *the* hell was that?" Cindy asked, marveling at the view of their backs as the militia squad flees.

Ritter holds up a glittering gemstone the size of a peach.

"Direct transmutation charm I've been working on with Ryland," he explains. "Swaps the metal in the shells with the flesh of the poor fuck firing the weapon."

"You could've warned me!" Moon shrieks at him.

"Yeah," Ritter says dryly. "I could've."

He tosses the gemstone to Moon.

Moon doesn't even try to catch it.

Ritter walks toward the baffled squad leader. The man's eyes are wide, and a war between confusion and fear is being fought in each blown pupil.

He goes for the pistol holstered on his belt.

As the man's hand closes around the grip of the pistol Ritter's left leg becomes a sudden blur, its shin breaking that hand in four places.

Ritter's opposite leg goes airborne almost before his

left leg touches back down. It travels in a perfect, lightning-fast crescent, driving its foot and most of its ankle into the side of the squad leader's face and skull.

He never makes a sound, not even when his body hits the grass-speckled dirt.

Ritter crouches down and removes his pistol, disassembling it quickly and expertly.

As he does, he flicks his chin at the stolen cargo on the back of the militia's jeep. "Let's get all of this shit back to the tribe and then get out of here."

"Can I at least rinse myself off first, for chrissakes?" Moon whines.

Ritter shrugs. "Do what you feel."

"Tell you the truth the smell is kind of a wash for you," Cindy informs him.

"Fuck you all."

Even Hara laughs at that.

EMPLOYMENT CONTRACT

Lena holds her right hand an inch above the surface of the large French omelet pan. The fire beneath it is stoked to capacity.

She waits until the rising heat threatens to blister her flesh.

That's the only way she trusts that it's ready.

Her small mise en place is militarily arranged beside the modest stovetop she shares with Darren. From it she drops a pad of butter into the scorching pan and quickly spreads it around, coating the entire surface. In a bowl with a pair of chopsticks protruding from the top she's whipped two eggs with a healthy pinch of salt and a tiny pinch of smoked paprika.

Taking up the bowl, she pours the creamy-golden liquid into the pan before the butter has a chance to blacken.

The sizzle that follows is one life's most satisfying sounds, according to Lena.

When the egg mixture hits the brown-buttered surface it cooks solid almost immediately, appearing to float on top of the metal as it shivers and ripples. Lena grips the handle and tips the pan on its axis, forcing the still-cooking eggs to fold against the curve of the vessel.

She rolls the slightly runny egg skirt onto a plate and sprinkles fresh parsley, sage, and dill over it.

"Darren!"

She waits, and by now she knows exactly how long it'll take before he's fallen back to sleep after waking momentarily.

"Darren!" she yells again. "Food's up!"

Thirty seconds later Darren emerges from the entrance to the single stubby hallway of their apartment. One leg of the boxers in which he sleeps is rolled up to his hip, and the gold cross and Our Lady of Guadalupe medal he always wears are resting on his right shoulder. His slipper-covered feet (his mother sends him a new pair every single Christmas) shuffle disjointedly along as he scratches at his matted black hair.

He crumples himself onto a stool at the bar that serves as the divider between their living room and kitchen. She's already poured them each a glass of orange juice into which she's submerged three cherries.

She does that.

Lena adds a fork to the plate she's composed and sets it in front of him.

"Julia Child morning," he mumbles as he observes

the omelet.

"All we had was eggs," she explains.

Darren picks up his fork, separating a large piece of solidified egg with the edge of a prong. He skewers the bite, lifts it an inch from his lips, then sets the loaded fork back down on the plate, untouched, with a sigh.

He rubs his sleep-crusted eyes until they're five deeper shades of red.

"It was a dream, right?" he asks her.

He sounds groggy, but there's also a distinctly hopeful, almost pleading note behind the question.

"What was?"

Lena knows precisely what he's referring to.

His frown tells her he knows very well that she knows.

"You know it wasn't a dream," she says impatiently. "Stop acting like a goddamn five-year-old."

The insult rolls right off him, barely noticed. If anyone else said such a thing to him it would probably wreck Darren for a week, but he knows Lena's judgment never equals rejection, at least where he's concerned.

"An angel," Darren says, still mystified. "A real angel."

"Yeah."

Another memory hits him, and his eyes go wide.

"And the dog!" he practically yells. "That dog, he was actually G—"

"I don't want to talk about what the fucking dog was or wasn't!" Lena snaps at him. "And keep your voice down!"

Darren deflates.

Lena pours another egg mixture into her pan and tips it, forming a second omelet for herself.

"It happened," she states with finality as she dresses the egg dish. "It happened, it was real. We were there. Just accept it and move on."

Darren sulks in silence, picking at his omelet without taking a bite.

"Eat that shit or you're going to wear it," Lena warns him as she drops her own plate on the counter and begins devouring it in military fashion.

Darren takes a bite.

"This is good."

"I know."

Darren wolfs the rest of the omelet down.

"So," he says, cautiously, after he's finished. "Are we going back?"

Lena very nearly chokes on a cherry from her orange juice glass. She stares angrily at him over the rim, swallowing it down almost whole before she replaces the glass on the counter.

She stares at Darren as if they've only just met. "Are you fucking kidding me?"

"What?"

There's a knock at their door.

Lena looks over at it, then picks up her phone and taps the big button, reading the current time.

She looks back at Darren. "You gave the old bitch our rent check, right?"

He nods.

Lena exits the barely-a-kitchenette and walks to the front door. She has to squint to identify anyone through the jungle of scratches over its exterior peephole.

At first she doesn't recognize the nondescript man in the black-and-white Adidas running suit, wondering if he's a jogger who has lost his cell phone or something.

Then a name leaps at her from the shadows of her own mind like a tiger, and Lena almost recoils in the same way.

Allensworth.

His name is Allensworth.

He's the man who delivered Ramiel, the captured angel, to Sin du Jour.

He's the man who expected them to serve every part of it at a banquet for demons.

He's the man who explained that expectation as if he were asking for a cup of sugar from a neighbor.

Lena turns away from the door.

"Oh, shit."

"What?" Darren asks from his barstool.

"It's the guy."

"What guy?"

"I don't know! He works for the government or the Devil or who the fuck knows? The *guy*, Darren!"

"Oh," Darren says before it actually hits him. "Oh! Oh, no!"

Lena hasn't felt this frantic or out of control since the first time her base camp came under fire from their unseen enemies in the desert.

"Miss Tarr," Allensworth calls to her from the other side of the door, his voice not at all elevated and entirely audible, "a less forthright individual would probably forgo revealing to you that your voices carry quite clearly into this hallway. I can't in good conscience stand mute, however."

Lena shuts her eyes tightly.

Her lips silently form a stream of the worst curses she can call to mind.

Darren opens his mouth to say something then snaps it shut and just shakes his head.

Lena turns around and opens the door.

As she does, it dawns on Darren how clothed he's not and he dashes from the barstool and down their apartment hallway.

Allensworth stands there, smiling cordially. He's

holding the end of a fine leather leash in one hand. The other end of the leash is connected to the collar of an adult Rottweiler, which sits obediently on the floor of the hallway, tongue hanging down from its mouth.

"What's that?" Lena asks suspiciously.

"That's Bruno. My dog. I was taking him for a walk. I actually don't live very far from here."

"Is he . . . is it . . . ?"

Allensworth tilts his head, brow furrowing with detached confusion.

"Never mind," Lena says quickly, shaking her head. "What do you want?"

Allensworth smiles, reaching up with his free hand and unzipping the jacket of his running suit.

He reaches inside its folds.

Lena's grip on the door tenses as she prepares to slam it in his face, her mind already listing and mapping the location of every nearby object that can be utilized in combat.

Instead she relaxes as he removes a thin sheaf of official-looking documents from inside his jacket and extends them toward her.

Lena looks down at the first page without taking it.

"What's this?" she asks, dubious.

"Your employment contracts."

At that moment Darren emerges from the back of

their apartment, still fitting a North Harrison High School Lacrosse jersey down around his waist.

"Employment contracts?"

"Good morning, Mister Vargas," Allensworth greets him.

"We didn't ask for these," Lena says quickly. "We didn't agree to—"

"Miss Tarr, I'm simply a messenger this morning. I am not . . . or will not be . . . your employer. Your employer, prospective or otherwise, is Sin du Jour. Your boss would or will be Byron Luck. You'll have to take the matter up with him in either case."

Allensworth gently tugs at Bruno's leash.

The Rottweiler stands at attention by his side, immediately.

"I will say," the strangely polite man adds, "we were all very impressed with how you . . . the both of you . . . comported yourselves on what must've been a very trying first day."

He leaves the doorway then, tugging Bruno along behind him and the dog trotting obediently.

It's a few seconds before it occurs to Lena to shut the door.

FINAL INTERVIEW

Bronko is approving purchase orders and debating what type of sandwich to make in the kitchen for his lunch when Lena storms his office without knocking.

Later he'll decide on heirloom tomato and pancetta on garlic toast.

She strides and stomps across the room and slaps the employment contracts down in the middle of his desk.

"What the hell is this supposed to be?"

"Did you sign and initial them all?" Bronko asks, unperturbed.

Lena isn't prepared for that. She's mustered all of herself to so starkly confront a chef of his position and caliber. She expected hell in return.

"What? I . . . what? No! Why would you think we'd sign these?"

Bronko thumbs through the unsigned sheaf of papers and leans back.

"I thought I'd hired you and Vargas. Maybe I'm gettin' old."

Lena is deflated, or at least the mad-on she'd worked

up so dutifully is.

"Chef," she says, much quieter, almost pleading, "I can't—"

"Are you speaking for yourself, or are you speaking for you and Vargas?"

Lena opens her mouth to answer, but before she can speak Bronko peers around her at his empty doorway and shouts, "Vargas! Are you out there?"

There's no reply at first.

Then, meekly, Darren's head appears around the side of the doorjamb like some absurd vaudeville skit.

"Yeah, Chef?"

"Get in here, for chrissakes, will you? Don't let people do your talkin' for you unless they're your agent. Is Tarr copping ten percent of your checks?"

"No, Chef."

"Well, then?"

Darren tentatively enters the room.

Bronko regards them both, silently.

Lena isn't sure what to say next.

"All right," he pronounces heavily, dropping both thick hands atop his desk, "here's the deal. You both did good, stepping up when I needed you to. It was only supposed to be a temporary gig. If you want, that's how it'll stay."

Bronko opens his top desk drawer and removes a narrow manila envelope, the center of which is bulging.

He plops it down beside the contracts.

It makes enough of a thud to get their attention.

"This is your payout for the days you worked here, plus event pay, plus hazard pay, plus a bonus for you, Tarr, because you helped Nikki and me tweak what needed tweaking with the menu for the banquet."

Lena's lips tighten, as does something in her gut. Somehow, Bronko not saying she helped them come up with how to fake dishes that were supposed to contain parts of an angel to be served to demons is even worse than him saying it outright.

"You can have it now and walk," Bronko continues. "In cash. Off the books. Or you sign these contracts for one year with a three-month probationary period for the amount outlined. Did you happen to look at what your salary will be?"

Lena folds her arms across her chest. "No."

"She totally did," Darren says without hesitation. "We both did. A lot."

Lena turns on him. "Goddammit, Darren."

"Principles or no principles," Darren insists, trying to sound hard and failing, "we're broke, El, and Chef knows it."

"I looked," Lena admits through clenched teeth. "It's a lot. Especially for us at the moment."

"It's *three times* what you'll make at any restaurant in Manhattan," Bronko assures them as Lena's eyes fall on the figure. "And that's as sous-chefs, let alone working the line."

It's enough to give even Lena pause, but the skeptical bent to her features doesn't relent.

"I'm not going to pitch you," Bronko says. "For one I'm no damn good at it, and for another neither of you has earned the right to be courted. You're good enough for the line. That's all. And that means a little something extra at Sin du Jour. And the truth is . . . we need you right now. We're prepping for a big event that's going to require extra hands on deck."

"What is it?" Darren asks.

"A wedding."

Lena's eyes narrow. "What kind of . . . wedding?"

"Goblins," Bronko answers simply.

Darren actually lights up. "Goblins like *Lord of the Rings*? Those kinds of goblins?"

"No."

"But it's a goblin wedding?"

"It's *the* goblin wedding," Bronko corrects him.

Lena lowers the contract in her hands.

She looks at Darren, whose expression is that of a child silently beseeching a parent to stop the car as they pass a toy store.

Lena looks back across the desk at Bronko.

"Okay. If they aren't *Lord of the Rings* goblins," she begins carefully, "just what exactly are they?"

THE MOST BEAUTIFUL OF
GOD'S CREATURES

Lena realizes Boosha's workroom is less apothecary and more an arcane test kitchen—one that would've existed long before the concept of a "test kitchen" itself. It is a room from a time when cooks were also healers, scientists, alchemists, barbers, and who-the-fuck-knows what else.

Not to mention the fact that Boosha herself is not entirely human.

Lena and Darren watch as the ancient woman rummages through piles of books that look as though they might've been bought in bulk to decorate the set of a Universal monster movie from the 1930s.

"Goblins are most beautiful of God's creatures by far," she explains. "I have a little goblin in me myself."

"Ma'am?" Darren asks.

Boosha turns and smiles a grandmotherly smile on him.

"I, uh, I've played a lot of D&D in my time—" he begins, nervously.

"He has," Lena confirms. "A pathetic amount."

"Goblins are monsters," Darren finishes sharply, eyeing her.

"Hm. What is 'monster'?"

"Uh, well, 'monster' is a word that means—"

"I know what word means," Boosha snaps. "I ask you what you think makes something monster."

"I . . . well, something big and ugly that probably eats babies? I don't know."

Boosha clicks her tongue, pulling out one of the dusty old volumes and slamming it against her carved wooden pedestal.

"Image of goblins you have comes from angry, jealous lies. Lies made by men and women. Jealous they were of goblin beauty, goblin spirit, goblin perfection. They wanted their sons and daughters to stop running off with goblins. So they spread lies, painted pictures. They made monsters of goblins."

"But if they *weren't* monsters why would people believe any of that?" Lena asks.

Boosha turns the brittle pages of the tome rapidly. "People were even more stupid back then. Ah, here we are."

She steps aside and motions for them both to examine the pages of the book.

The illustrations are old, faded, and crude. One page depicts children in their teens crawling, almost supplicating toward a lithe, luminous figure awaiting them with open arms.

The opposing page depicts the same young people in the same setting, only now they're being torn apart by a monstrous fanged creature where the luminous figure stands in the first illustration.

"But they don't turn into monsters?" Darren asks.

Boosha shakes her head.

"No. Mostly they are just very, very pretty. Their looks cast spell on most. Snare them. This is how they make their way in world. By their looks."

"How's that?"

"In past they were showpeople or thieves. Today they are in movies, mostly. All the very pretty people in movies are mostly goblin."

Darren's eyes are wide. "What, like George Clooney?"

Boosha shrugs.

"So what do they eat?" Lena asks impatiently. "These 'goblins' of yours."

Boosha makes a "cluck" sound with her tongue, but she lets Lena's tone slide.

"Gold is goblin delicacy."

"Gold what?"

"Gold," Boosha reiterates sharply.

"You mean like . . ."

Boosha reaches out and pinches the gold chain around Darren's neck between the tip of her thumb and forefinger.

She rattles the chain while enunciating slowly.

"Goooooollllld-da."

"Fine. They eat gold. I get it."

"How do you cook gold?" Darren asks.

"Carefully," is Boosha's only answer.

"So aside from being . . . whatever . . . goblins . . . what's so important about this wedding?"

Boosha stares at Lena as if she were the most ignorant of children in a classroom.

"Is royal wedding, dear," she explains patiently. "Goblin prince is to marry his princess. Goblin king will be here for tasting this very afternoon."

"Goblin king?" Darren marvels.

"Royal wedding," Lena says to herself more than Darren or the old woman.

Darren can't contain himself any longer.

"Who's the goblin king?" he practically explodes. "Who is it?"

A HINT OF STARDUST

"He looks like—"

"I know."

"But he looks *exactly* like—"

"Yeah. I know."

"But he can't be—"

"Sure he can."

"You don't mean—"

"Yes, I do mean."

"No fucking way."

"It's actually him?"

"It's him."

"But he . . . he played the Goblin King in that movie."

"Why do you think he took the part, kid?"

The chefs of Sin du Jour line the wall of the reception room like servants in the home of imperial Roman aristocracy. Each one dons their freshest whites emblazoned with the company logo, the walking, talking cartoon chocolate cake slice known among them as "Mr. Frosting Face."

Darren is standing shoulder-to-shoulder with Tag

Dorsky, Sin du Jour's sous-chef. Lena is trying to fade into the wall on Darren's opposite side. They're both wearing whites that look a size too big on their equally slight frames.

Dorsky is being surprisingly amiable with them both, considering it wasn't a week ago Lena slashed him open in two places with a paring knife during a duel out in the courtyard.

Maybe he's gotten over it.

Maybe he just wants to forget it.

More than likely he just wants to forget it.

The goblin king's immaculate, slightly lupine features are kind, but reserved. A designer with an eighteen-syllable name undoubtedly made his suit, and it hangs stunningly on his slender frame. His hair, which has gone through so many famous and kaleidoscopic changes on decades of album covers, is now a simple, chemically flawless blond that falls loosely just past his ears.

He's a beautiful man, even for someone who is supposed to be almost seventy in human years and who is god-only-knows how old in goblin years.

The queen is several inches taller than him, skin perfectly bronzed, perfectly smooth, and just generally perfect. She looks even more ageless than he does.

She's also one of the most famous supermodels in history.

Lena can scarcely process what's happening. It would be enough to find herself in the same room with these people when she thought they were simply celebrities and entertainment-industry royalty. Now she knows they're not human. They're goblins. More than that, they are the rulers of some invisible goblin kingdom that has infiltrated and conquered the highest levels of all popular media.

It's a little much for a girl on a Monday morning.

Lena can see Darren has chosen to ignore the more fantastical aspects of the moment. He's simply in awe of a legendary singer and a legendary model.

She decides he has the right idea. In fact, faced with too much to process, Lena simply shuts her brain down altogether.

Besides, there's food.

There's a long, narrow buffet table set up in the middle of the reception room, draped with a shimmering crimson cloth. Jett excitedly leads the royal family to one end of it, looking more animated and joyful than Lena has yet seen the out-of-place Chanel-clad event planner.

There are two much younger people accompanying the goblin king and queen.

The first is obviously their son, the prince, whose eyes are so kind and open they actually stand out against his inhumanly attractive and symmetrical features.

The other is his bride-to-be, a cordial young woman who is very pretty, possibly even beautiful, but looks, like everyone else in the room, thoroughly ordinary in the presence of these physically extraordinary goblins.

"All right, Your Majesties," Jett announces brightly, "this is, of course, the world famous Chef Byron Luck, our fearless leader in the kitchen here at Sin du Jour. And this is Nichole Glowin, his pastry chef."

Bronko and Nikki stand on the other side of the table. Arrayed before them is what looks to be a Japanese meal progression of thoroughly Western food. Tiny portions of a dozen different dishes are plated meticulously in a perfectly spaced row, each with a delicate knife and fork or spoon beside it resting atop fine linen napkins.

"Please, call me Bronko," the executive chef says in his easy way.

"Nikki," she says, raising her hand as if she's in a classroom, then adding hastily, "Your Majesties."

"It's a pleasure to meet you both," the goblin king says. "My luminous wife, the queen, and our son, Marek. This is his betrothed, Bianca."

Introductions are made all the way around.

"What we have for you today," Bronko begins, clapping his hands together in that way chefs who've been on television a lot do, "is a tasting of the dual menu we've planned for your wedding. It's been made clear to us everything must be prepared two ways, yes?"

"Unavoidably so," the king remarks, pleasantly enough. "Watching humans attempt to digest goblin fare is a harrowing sight, indeed."

The queen laughs, demurely.

The prince tries to, but manages only a smile.

Bianca doesn't make it that far.

"Right. Well," Bronko continues, "we'll have a full precious metals and jewels station for the groom's relations to snack on. Likewise, our servers will make the rounds with hors d'oeuvres gems and pearls. For the bride's side of the aisle we've prepared cherry pepper bruschetta..."

Bronko takes them through samples of the hors d'oeuvres, appetizers, and four starting dinner courses they've planned out. All three members of the royal family eat heartily of the "human" dishes (apparently, Lena observes, they can and do enjoy regular food).

"Finally," Bronko trumpets with appropriate grandeur, "we have our main course."

A medium-sized whole fish rests on each plate. The heads have been left intact. They've all been covered with gold semicircles. It looks as though each entrée is wearing plate armor.

"You're obviously familiar with the cultural significance and its importance to our goblin guests."

"Absolutely. Of course, we haven't actually used the ancestor fish for this tasting. We want to keep the actual product fresh for the reception. It's, as you know, getting rarer and harder to attain with each passing century."

"Yes, I know it's a silly tradition. Goblins descending from that hideous sea-dwelling creature. But we have so few pure goblin traditions left, you see."

"Which is why so many of our guests feel put out by a dual menu. Catering to humans, you know."

The queen says this casually, her tone implying she feels neither one way nor another about it, but the words have a noticeable affect on Bianca.

Bronko diplomatically brushes past the comments. "Your entrée is also prepared two ways, first with the traditional goldmail. The second preparation substitutes cucumber glazed with a rich yellow wasabi dressing for your human guests."

Against the wall, Darren and Lena exchange mystified looks.

The wasabi-drenched cucumbers look identical to the genuine gold plating on the opposite fish.

"Yellow wasabi," Lena mouths silently.

Darren shrugs.

"I don't know about the gold, but this with the cucumbers is amazing," Bianca says as she devours several forkfuls of the fish.

Bronko dips his head briefly. "Thank you, ma'am."

"This is domestic," His Majesty observes after a single bite of his gold-plated fish.

"Domestic, with a hint of a Hishikari I think," his wife adds.

"I think you're right, my love."

For the first time during the tasting, Bronko is thrown off his game. "I'm sorry, Your Majesty?"

"The presentation is quite lovely, as are the flavors, but the dish will of course be Welsh gold when you prepare it for our guests. Money is no object. It's not only expected, but anticipated for an event such as this."

"Oh, certainly," Bronko assures His Majesty without the slightest hesitation or hint not knowing what the hell he means by "Welsh" gold, or what the difference is.

The goblin king nods. "Very well. I'd say we approve wholeheartedly of the savory fare, Chef."

The queen nods in agreement. "Quite. Kids?"

Prince Marek and Bianca both nod rapidly, clasping each other's hand.

"All right then, folks." Bronko motions to the end of the table. "This is the fun part. Cake."

Nikki waits for them at the end of the table, behind an assortment of plated cake pieces. Each piece has a rich, vibrant red interior surrounded by white frosting that's as perfectly smooth as fondant, but looks far too rich and soft to be the decorative sheet frosting that usually covers elaborate cakes.

Each piece is also sparkling brilliantly in the light, as if they're covered with diamonds.

"I love your hair," the goblin queen comments as they join Nikki across her end of the table.

"Oh, thank you," Nikki says, involuntarily touching one of the several victory rolls being held with bobby pins. "It's actually really easy to do."

"I was sorry to see it ever go out of fashion."

"I . . . yes." Nikki isn't sure what else to say, as the implication the woman has been around since her hairstyle was at the height of its popularity in the '40s hits her.

"Well then, Nikki," the king interjects. "Do tell us about cake."

"Oh. Of course. First, for the . . . groom's side of the aisle, what I've done is created a ruby jam center. The frosting is silky pearl, both white and black, which we've blended. And it's sprinkled with blue diamond chips."

Lena can't believe the description.

Ruby jam?

Frosting made from pearls?

"How the hell—" she begins, catching herself quickly.

No one seems to notice.

Everyone except Bianca takes up a fork. Soon an inhuman crunching of jaws fills the room.

"That is utterly magnificent," the king says without hesitation.

The queen and prince are quick to agree.

Nikki's smile spreads with genuine delight.

"Thank you. And for the bride's side, we have blood orange cake with a frosting of vanilla bean ganache. The sprinkles are crushed hard candy made from sea salt, taro, and blue agave."

"Jesus, they look identical," Lena can't help whispering.

Fortunately only Darren and Dorsky hear her.

Darren nudges her.

Dorsky smirks without looking past him at Lena.

Nikki picks up a fork and offers it to Bianca, who has been standing to one side trying not to look uncomfortable.

The young woman steps forward, seeming to appreciate the gesture. She takes the fork and bisects a good-sized bite from the blood orange cake, bringing it to her lips and sniffing it demurely.

"It smells amazing," she says.

Nikki nods enthusiastically. "I know, right?"

Bianca takes her first bite of her wedding cake.

Her first words, to Nikki's mind, are perfect: "Babe," she says, forking another bite for the prince, "you've got to try this. It's amazing."

"Which of these will be the cake that's presented to our guests?" His Highness inquires.

"Oh, we'll be constructing a beautiful veneer," Jett chimes in quickly. "Over two stories tall. Identical in every fashion to the outside of the real thing, and absolutely elaborate and stunning, but the center will be hollow."

"Giant cakes taste like they came from a supermarket," Bronko assures the goblin king. "Your guests will be eating much smaller, much higher quality versions."

His Highness nods. "You've done well, Chef Luck," he congratulates Bronko with a lupine smile, reaching out and clasping both of the man's larger, far more battered hands with his own.

Bronko is surprised by the strength contained in those seemingly delicate, manicured hands, but he doesn't let it show.

"Thank you. Your Majesty."

"And Nikki, you are truly gifted," the queen adds. "Both as a pastry chef and a hair stylist."

"Oh, it's nothing, really."

The goblin king turns toward the rest of the line.

"I thank you all!"

Darren almost giggles with excitement, but manages to hold it in.

"Your Majesty," Jett bids them. "If you'll follow me

I've prepared a preview of our designs for the space, the lighting, and of course the music . . ."

Jett is already free-flowing ecstatically with her event ideas as she leads them from the room.

"What do you think?" Bronko asks Nikki after a safe amount of time.

"That poor girl," she says automatically.

"The food, Nik."

"Oh! They liked it."

Bronko nods.

The rest of the line cooks begin filing out of the room while Dorsky approaches the table.

"Welsh gold?" he asks.

Bronko shrugs. "How hard can it be?"

Darren, his eyes glued to the Wikipedia page he's conjured on his iPhone, answers that very rhetorical question: "It's the rarest gold in the world, Chef."

Dorsky frowns.

"Well." Bronko takes a deep breath. "He did say money was no object."

With a deep, doubtful grunt, his sous-chef turns and exits the reception room.

Bronko waits.

"So, what's the verdict?" he asks Lena when they're alone.

Lena pulls at her chef whites.

"Can we get these fitted?"

"So that's a yes?"

"We'll try it."

"Yeah, we will," Bronko says heavily. "You're both on three months' probation, after which a peer review will determine whether or not your employment contracts fully activate."

"Peer meaning who?" Darren asks.

"The rest of the line."

"Dorsky," Lena states flatly.

Bronko nods.

"Great."

"Just focus on the next couple of weeks, children," Bronko advises them. "The first two weeks are the most important. You make it past that, the rest is clerical. Is 'clerical' the right word?"

"You're our executive chef," Lena says flatly. "Even if it isn't the right word it is the right word."

Bronko grins. "See that? You're gonna do just fine. We'll get you some fitted whites and make sure you sign your contracts before you leave today. All right?"

"Yes, Chef."

Bronko looks to Darren.

"Yes, Chef," he says quickly.

"Good."

Bronko turns and exits the room.

"You look great," Nikki says to Lena with a smile.

"No, I don't."

"No, but you will."

"How the hell did you make a jam out of rubies?"

"Is that why you agreed to take the job?" Nikki asks her.

Lena is hesitant. "Mostly."

"The money didn't hurt?" Nikki asks knowingly.

"It didn't hurt, no."

GRANDDAD WAS A MEDICINE MAN

Bronko tasks Jett with giving them a full tour of the facilities. When they first entered Sin du Jour as temps, Darren and Lena were only shown their own workspace. Even after their involvement in the ruse with the angel, Ramiel, whom they did not serve as planned to the Oexial and Vig'nerash demon clans at the banquet to celebrate a treaty between the two.

"One of you has already learned this the hard way," Bronko tells them with a hard eye on Darren before relinquishing them to Jett's care, "but this can be a dangerous place to go a-wandering. Best you start familiarizing yourselves with it now."

They soon realize Sin du Jour is more like four separate buildings mashed together around a large courtyard. And the way the complex connects from wing to wing doesn't meet any standard of architectural common sense.

"I didn't realize this place was so big," Darren marvels.

"The façade is fairly recent," Jett explains. "The rest of

the brick structures are all prewar."

"What were they before Sin du Jour moved in?" Lena asks.

Jett halts briefly.

"As far as I know Sin du Jour has always been here," she muses, more to herself than them. "But I . . . hmmmmmm . . ."

She banishes whatever thoughts halted her feet with a shrug and leads on.

"You'll mostly stick to the main kitchen in the north wing. Sometimes if the event is big enough we'll overflow into some of the satellite kitchens, but it's rare."

She leads them past a massive vertical steel slab on rails. A thick chain lock tethers one side to the wall.

Someone has painted across it, sloppily: "Alright Shamblers Let's Get Shamblin.'"

"Please forgive and ignore the graffiti," Jett urges them, obviously annoyed. "The uneven hand would suggest Ryland, but he isn't given to American pop culture references. My guess would be Moon."

She removes the lock with a large key kept on an elegant chain around her neck. Jett clamps two hands on the slab's handle and, quite impressively for someone under five feet five inches tall and wearing Christian Louboutin heels, yanks what turns out to be a door aside with brute force and a yell.

"There we go," she says, smoothing her Chanel suit and smiling at them anew.

Inside is what looks very much like a children's playroom.

A children's playroom designed for zombies.

The large space is filled with simple games, large toys, the clinking of heavy chains, and dozens upon dozens of the undead clad in Sin du Jour–logo work coveralls.

They all appear docile enough from across the threshold. There's some gentle moaning and groaning, but most of them appear content to kick at or gnaw on large rubber balls and stuffed animals.

"This is my staff's employee lounge," Jett explains brightly. "Never, under any circumstance, open or otherwise tamper with this door. And needless to say, do not enter. Are there any questions?"

"This is pretty fucked up," Lena bluntly states.

The comment doesn't even faze Jett. "That's not precisely a question, but in response I'd point out that they all died in unrelated accidents, most of them in Los Angeles. Their families continue to receive what equates to each of their salaries as 'insurance' payouts. They possess no self-awareness we've been able to measure via technological or mystical means. They're meat with a trace amount of instinct reverberation, which makes them suited to event planning."

Neither Lena nor Darren can muster a retort.

In fact, Lena's not sure Darren heard of any of that, as shell-shocked as he appears.

"Moving on." Jett slams the door home and relocks it. She leads them onward.

"Now, in addition to the other chefs, my event planning staff, and the stocking and receiving department, whom you've met, we also employ several practitioners of the more metaphysical arts and sciences. You know Boosha, of course."

"Yeah," Lena says. "What is she, exactly?"

"Eccentric," Jett answers immediately and without further explanation. "But she's the most knowledgeable member of the staff when it comes to arcane and otherworldly cuisines. I'll introduce you to Ryland Phelan, our resident alchemist, at the end of the tour, but for now . . ."

She leads them to a suite of offices in what Lena thinks is the west wing of the complex, but she's not even close to certain by this point.

The offices are clean, well appointed, and decorated largely with Navajo folk art, including several shallow boards filled with raked sand that seem less like decoration and more haphazardly strewn about several points in the suite. Most of it is thematically consistent, with the exception of a dominating Ke$ha poster on the wall above the empty reception desk.

It's the second most distracting feature of the suite, with the first being the ancient-looking individual napping on a leather sofa as they enter. He's got two small buds twisted into each ear, connected to an iPod on his stomach.

Lena recognizes the old Native American man from the kitchen, immediately after the episode with the creature from the pantry that took Ritter's arm off. He was chanting around a large spill of flour with designs drawn in it on the floor of the kitchen, beside a much younger woman.

He looks exactly the way a twenty-three-year-old who has only seen Navajos in movies would expect him to look: faded jeans, scuffed and worn cowboy boots, a jacket made from elk's hide, and a shocking mane of white hair.

"Mister White Horse?" Jett ventures softly.

"No 'mister,' little lady," the old man says without opening his eyes or removing the earbuds. "I've told you that before."

"Yes, sir. I just wanted to introduce Lena Tarr and Darren Vargas. They're our new chefs."

"Charmed."

White Horse rolls over on the sofa, away from them.

Darren and Lena look at Jett.

She continues to smile with all the poise in the world.

Fortunately a young woman, around Lena and Darren's age, comes sprinting out of the back room. She's obviously of tribal descent, but she's less the stereotype from the movies in her midriff top and checkered miniskirt.

Lena recognizes the boots she has on from Torrid.

"I didn't hear you guys come in!" she says, smiling at the trio.

"Ah!" Jett is obviously relieved. "This is Little Dove . . . White Horse's assistant. She's also his granddaughter."

"Just call me Lill," she says to Darren and Lena, shaking both of their hands.

"Your mother didn't name you 'Lill,' you shameful apple of a girl," White Horse says from the sofa without turning over.

Little Dove's smile never wavers, although they can all see that it's an effort to maintain it.

"Thanks for that, Pop," she says.

"Apple?" Darren asks.

"Red on the outside, white on the inside," she explains, trying to be jovial about it. "He's a very, very old man."

"Oh."

"I'm sorry, what is it you and your grandfather do here again?" Lena asks.

"Landscaping?" Darren offers without sarcasm, looking around at the various sand paintings.

"Mist—. . . uh . . . White Horse here is a sort of a . . . well, wizard, I suppose," Jett explains brightly.

The old man snorts derisively at that.

"A wizard is what they were in the market for," Little Dove corrects her. "Unfortunately 'wizards' aren't much to be found in a country that's two hundred years old and change."

"My country is ageless," White Horse points out.

"I know, Pop," she placates the old man. Then, to the rest of them: "Point is, if you want a wizard you have to import one from across an ocean. They're a Middle English concept. If you want American magic, a Hatałii is pretty much your oldest, best, and most powerful bet."

"A hata-whatta?" Darren stammers.

On the sofa, White Horse spreads his arms ceremoniously, still never opening his eyes. "I am a medicine man, my son! Come to me and I will lay trembling hands upon you!"

"Pop, cut it out!" Little Dove snaps at him.

The old man laughs, rolling back over.

"Chef Luck likes to keep a veteran magic-user on staff," Jett offers. "A lot of the fare you'll work with and prepare contains . . . properties that can go a bit haywire if not treated properly. White Horse uses his skills in a preventative capacity."

Darren nods like he understands completely.

Lena stares at him like he's just passed gas.

"And they called my people crazy," White Horse mutters.

Little Dove leans close. "Look, it's not as weird as it sounds. We're like, you know, the FDA. We make sure the food won't kill anybody. Don't worry."

"Oh, I feel much better," Lena assures her.

"Well, then," Jett says. "Thank you for your time, folks. Darren, Lena, if you'll follow me."

"Hey," Little Dove says, "come hang later when you get a break if you want. I'm stuck back here all day tending to him. It gets . . . yeah."

"Sure," Darren offers, warmly.

Lena only nods.

"Nice to meet you both," she says.

Little Dove smiles at her. "You too."

As Jett leads them down the hallway outside the suite, they can all hear Little Dove yelling at her grandfather and White Horse laughing.

Only Darren and Lena seem to acknowledge the sounds, however.

INTRODUCTIONS WITH ALL LIMBS ATTACHED

James, the Senegalese line cook who Lena remembers as the only other member of the kitchen staff besides Nikki who stood with them against Dorsky, escorts them to an immaculately clean and surprisingly homey changing room complete with lockers.

"We do not have separate space for the boys and the girls," James apologetically explains.

"It's fine," Lena says, trying not to let her tone become too jagged, aware he's being sincere.

He leads them to the last row of lockers facing the wall.

"Take two here. You will have privacy back here."

"Thanks, man," Darren says.

They both choose a locker and pull open their respective doors.

Inside each new chef whites embroidered with their first names are hanging neatly on miniature hangers.

"Holy crap," Darren marvels.

Lena's voice is suspicious. "What the hell? Are these for us? How did they get here so fast?"

James only shrugs.

"They will fit, I expect," he says. "Change yourselves and join us on the line, okay?"

Lena just nods.

"Thanks," Darren says again, smiling.

James smiles back at him.

Lena waits, and her waiting more than anything else is what marks the moment their exchange of smiles officially passes friendly into awkward.

Lena clears her throat.

Both Darren and James look away in a hurry.

James leaves them, whistling to himself.

"Do you think it's, like, magic?" Darren asks when he's gone. "The chef whites?"

"Shut up," Lena snaps.

"What?" he asks her innocently.

Lena rips her new fitted personalized chef whites from the hanger and straddles the bench between the lockers and the wall. She removes the temporary smock Bronko gave her and slips on the embroidered uniform.

It fits perfectly.

"Son of a bitch," she whispers.

She's leaning over to stuff her things inside the locker when a voice that doesn't belong to Darren speaks her name.

"It's Lena, right?"

She didn't hear anyone else enter the room.

Lena peers around the locker door at Ritter.

"Yeah. Hi."

Ritter looks over at Darren. "You two are full-time now?"

He nods.

"Probationary period," Lena says.

Ritter looks back at her. "Right. Look, I know you signed up at a weird time, even for this place, but once you get into the routine it all normalizes. It can be hard, coming from the straight world."

"Which world do you come from?" Lena asks him, more defensively than she meant to and not caring.

"It . . . had a little less padding around it," Ritter answers carefully.

"Dude. You don't know where we come from," Lena snaps at him.

"The Midwest—" Darren begins.

"Darren!" she hisses.

Ritter only nods, undisturbed. "True enough. Just so you know, it starts to feel less weird."

"Thanks. Did you come here just to tell me that?"

"No. It occurred to me I never thanked you. I thanked your partner here, but as I recall it was him cradling my arm and you cradling everything else."

Ritter holds up the appendage that was not attached to his body when he and Lena first met.

Lena doesn't answer at first, only blinking rapidly in surprise. She wasn't expecting that.

In truth, with everything that had happened since the moment she found herself holding Ritter and trying to keep him conscious she'd either lost it or blocked it out.

"I . . . I just happened to be the one standing closest to you. Don't worry about it."

"Well, you're a hell of a field medic."

"Thanks."

"You were in the service, right?"

Lena nods. "Yeah. Army. You?"

"I served."

She waits.

"So? Where?"

For the first time, Ritter grins. There's something bittersweet there, perhaps mostly bitter, and clearly not intended for her.

"No outfit you've ever heard of," is all he says.

Her first instinct is to say something glib, but something about the way he smiled stops her. It's as if he were remembering a million troublesome moments all at once.

"Anyway. Thanks again for the assist. Hopefully I

won't have to return the solid someday."

Ritter leaves them with that.

Darren watches him go.

Lena makes a point of not watching him go.

Darren is idly toying with one of the buttons on his new chef whites. "You don't think he might be—"

"I honestly couldn't tell you. I can't read anyone in this fucking madhouse."

"Right. Yeah. He's got a nice cover, though."

Lena looks up at him blankly.

"You know," Darren mumbles. "Read. Book. Cover." A pause. "He's hot."

She shifts her gaze back to her new smock.

"That permanent five o'clock shadow thing is such a cliché," Lena grumbles.

"For a reason."

Lena doesn't respond to that for several moments.

Then, begrudgingly: "Point."

Darren grins.

Lena tries to frown at him, but ends up grinning back.

"All right, nerd," she says. "Let's go to work."

"Yes, Chef."

PART II

THE SECRET INGREDIENT

WEEK-AND-A-HALF

A professional kitchen is all about routine and mechanical efficiency.

Lena and Darren are finding out this remains true even when you cook for demons and goblins.

They're spending every hour of their probationary period on the line in Sin du Jour's kitchen preparing hors d'oeuvres and appetizers for the royal wedding, which is scheduled to take place just after that probationary period ends. For the first few days, in fact, they weren't even allowed to cook. They spent their hours polishing tiny, bite-sized gemstones and precious metals for the free-standing jewel stations (which Jett explained to them in what seemed like endless detail) the goblin guests will be snacking on during cocktail hour.

Now they're replicating the starter menu for over one thousand guests, which means preparing several times that many of each dish.

The tedium and constant repetition of the line still gets to Darren. His eyes blur and his head aches and his mind screams for a break in the routine. It's a struggle to stay focused, to make each dish a perfect mirror image of the last.

When Darren was eight years old Tio Napoleon came to live with them from Xalapa. He was a line cook, and he quickly took over the small kitchen in their home. The food he prepared for them was unlike anything Darren had ever eaten, exploding with color and spice and flavor. Napoleon always sang when he cooked; loudly and soulfully, and always in Spanish, which Darren's mother only spoke on the phone to relatives.

It looked like the most fun Darren could imagine anyone having doing anything.

It made him want to become a chef.

Darren still loves cooking, but he has never once sung on the line.

The repetition never seems to faze Lena. She trains that laser focus of hers on each dish, replicating it meticulously and perfectly, seeming to find new challenges in the task, no matter how many times she's performed it already that day.

Darren admires, even envies that in her.

It also annoys the piss out of him.

"You're doing good, kid," Dorsky informs him abruptly as Darren folds uncooked puff pastry around a lobster and mushroom filling for the three-hundred-and-fifty-first time.

Darren looks over at him, surprised, even slightly alarmed.

Dorsky and his rotund lieutenant, Rollo, who seems to have frizzy hair sprouting from every exposed patch of skin on his body, are attending to prep the wedding's dinner menu.

"What, Chef?" Darren asks, as if he hasn't heard correctly.

"You're keeping those Wellington edges consistent," Dorsky says without looking up from his station. "I like seeing that. Keep it up, Vargas."

"Uh. Thanks, Chef."

Lena casts a suspicious, sidelong glance Dorsky's way, her hands never ceasing their work.

"I need more shutes for the meatball lollipops," Darren announces a time later.

"Rollo, take him to the pantry. Make sure he stays out of the restricted section this time."

Rollo and the rest of the kitchen laugh at that.

Darren tries to hide his embarrassment.

Poorly.

"C'mon, young'n," the bear of a man bids him.

When Rollo escorts Darren off the line Lena and Dorsky are left alone on their side of the kitchen.

The silence, even to a deeply unobservant person, can only be classified as "oppressive."

"You have something you want to say to me?" Dorsky asks, idly, concentrating on the several hundred gallons of Thai consommé for which he's prepping stock.

"No, Chef," Lena answers stiffly.

Dorsky grins. "Man, that must taste like shit in your mouth, having to call me that. C'mon, speak your mind."

"Fine." Lena sets her knife down and grabs a hand towel. "The way you're kissing his ass. Darren. What is that? A divide-and-conquer thing?"

Dorsky looks over at her then, and his eyes read genuinely confused. "What the hell are you talking about, Tarr?"

"If you're trying to get him on your side, or whatever, you should know we grew up together. We walked off our last job together when they tried to pull that kind of shit."

"I don't know what kind of shit you mean, and I don't know what happened on the last line you worked, but that's not how I do things."

"Then why are you being so goddamn nice to him?"

"Because he needs it."

"Then why are you still being such an ass to me? Why aren't you giving me that 'atta-boy' shit?"

"Because you don't need it."

Those two statements, and their underlying truth, throw Lena, but only for a moment.

"All right, then why were you such a dick to us the first

time we walked in here?"

"You weren't part of my line. You were just day-players trespassing in my kitchen."

"Uh-huh. And now?"

"You're part of my line."

He says it with a tone of such obviousness and finality that at first all Lena can manage to respond with is, "Oh."

They go back to working in silence.

Until Lena slams her knife down again.

"You know, that is such bullshit!"

Dorsky is actually caught off guard by the outburst.

She turns on him. "You can play that 'I'm just looking out for my boys' card, that's fine, but we both know it's no excuse for the way you act, the shit you say. Nikki is just as important to this kitchen as you are, and you were treating her like the enemy the second I walked in here."

Dorsky looks up from his stock, his eyes wider than she's yet seen them.

For the first time he stammers, "Listen ... first of all ... you don't know anything about me and Glowin. All right? Secondly ..."

Lena waits, and at first she's amused by the change in his demeanor, until it hits her how completely contrary it is to the usual bullshit bravado she's seen him exude.

She considers the possibility she made it over the wall for the briefest of moments.

"Yeah?" she asks, waiting, actually interested in what he's going to say next.

"Just concentrate on your prep," Dorsky finally says.

"Yes, Chef."

The word somehow tastes less bitter in her mouth this time.

BRIDE PROBLEMS

Lena, as she's made a habit of doing, is hanging out in the pastry kitchen with Nikki, marveling at the process by which she turns Burmese rubies into an edible jam.

Well, edible for goblins, anyway.

"Ryland is a miserable, insufferable little man," Nikki explains, "but he's a brilliant alchemist. He'd probably be a gagillionaire if he could lay off the booze and stop acting like such a prick for five minutes."

Lena laughs, loudly and genuinely.

It's the only time at work she does.

"Excuse me?" a delicate voice calls to them from the entrance to the pastry kitchen.

The turn to see Bianca, the goblin prince's fiancée, standing there, clutching her purse string in both hands before her awkwardly.

Nikki swallows, feeling suddenly exposed. "Princess Bianca! I didn't know you were in the building."

She smoothes her hands hopelessly over her stained apron.

Lena watches her, frowning slightly, lacking the instilled awe of goblin culture to feel impressed by the young woman's presence.

"Please," Bianca begs her. "I'm not a . . . princess."

"Not yet," Lena points out dryly.

Bianca smiles awkwardly. "Right."

"What's wrong?" Nikki asks, the woman's obvious pain overcoming Nikki's sense of propriety. "Come in, please. Would you like a cupcake?"

Her smile becomes a little easier.

She nods. "I kinda would, yeah."

Nikki invites the princess bride to sit at one of the kitchen's small islands. She retrieves one of her signature spumoni cupcakes, a few of which are always stowed away in one or more freezers, and plates it quickly for the woman.

The first bite seems to instantly, if briefly, overcome the young woman's emotional state.

"Ohmagod amazing," she says through a mouthful of chocolate mint chip–filled cherry cake and pistachio frosting.

Nikki grins happily.

Lena joins them at the island, having retrieved three wineglasses and a bottle of dessert wine.

"How can we help you?" Nikki asks sincerely.

"It's just . . . you were so nice at the tasting," Bianca explains. "And you looked like . . . like you kind of understood? And I don't really have anyone to talk to about this. My friends and my family . . . it's just a whole other world to them."

Lena snorts. "Tell me about it," she says, gulping down a glass of wine before either of them have reached for theirs.

Nikki shoots her a reprimanding look.

Lena shrugs apologetically.

"What's wrong?" Nikki asks Bianca. "Is it the wedding? The prince?"

"God, no. No." Bianca takes a sip of her wine. It seems to fortify her to go on. "Marek is amazing. Really. He's not . . . Goblins, the ones who live in the spotlight, they have their public families and their private families, see. So he grew up away from all of that. He's very smart and very down to earth. He's been groomed to rule and to lead. And that's what he is, a leader. But his family . . . and all of their friends . . ."

"Assholes?" Lena asks bluntly.

Bianca buries her face in her hands. "They hate me so much, you guys. I just can't even."

"Oh, honey." Nikki immediately slips her arm around Bianca's shoulders.

"And they're so cold about it!" she exclaims through tears. "That's the thing! If they'd, like, yell, or say shit to me, I could take that. But they just act so cold and formal and . . . so . . . fucking . . . tolerant! I hate it!"

Nikki progresses into full-blown hugging.

Lena responds by topping off Bianca's glass.

"I'm just worried I'll never feel like part of the family . . . or worse, part of their world. His world."

She sniffs and sips and then sips some more.

"I'm sorry to dump this on you. You don't even know me."

"It's cool," Lena says. "I kinda know what you're going through. All of this . . . other world stuff is new to me, too."

Bianca's eyes widen. "Really?"

Lena nods.

"But she's coping," Nikki points out.

Lena nods more fiercely. "I am."

Bianca breathes a little easier, if nothing else feeling less the freak in the room.

"Listen," Nikki says. "Your wedding is going to be amazing. The food is going to be spectacular. And that man loves you. We could both tell."

"And he is fucking gorgeous," Lena adds. "Like . . . ridiculous hot."

Bianca laughs at that. "Thank you . . . thank you both. I just . . . it was suffocating me. I just needed to vent."

"We get that," Nikki assures her. "Believe me."

The three of them talk and drink for another hour,

but the silent member of their conversation doesn't stay for the rest.

Boosha, listening so intently and so sympathetically at the door, has heard quite enough.

SECRET INGREDIENT

Sin du Jour is never really empty.

They regularly burn the midnight oil, sure, but it's more than that.

For some members of the staff Sin du Jour is more than a job, it's a home.

Bronko falls asleep at his desk so often he hasn't changed the sheets on his bed at home in six months.

Ryland, generally passed out by dusk inside or in front of his stationary RV out back, has long supplanted the need for any night watchperson.

And then there's Boosha, who literally has not left Sin du Jour in what seems like the span of a human lifetime.

She putters around quite happily in her apothecary/ test kitchen from dawn till dusk. She tastes the food of the "children," as she calls them. She dispenses wisdom and advice. She tells her stories.

No one ever sees her outside of her little corner of the complex.

But she does, occasionally, venture out.

It's nearly 3:00 in the morning. Everyone who has a

home to go to has left. Most of the building is dark and deathly quiet.

It's now that Boosha traipses silently into the cold storage, where a wealth of delicious fare for the royal goblin wedding awaits delivery.

She's carrying a large sack filled with a very rare herb ground to the finest powder.

"Poor girl," she whispers to herself as she begins sprinkling nearly imperceptible amounts of the powder over every single dish. "Poor, poor girl."

It takes her hours to seed the entire menu for the wedding reception.

But she doesn't miss a single scrap.

THE ROYAL GOBLIN WEDDING

It's your basic ridiculously opulent celebrity wedding reception.

Lena and Darren (mostly Darren) were expecting something more fantastical in a Tolkien-esque sense, but that's what it is. There's a red carpet, there's the latest fashions fresh off the runways of Milan and Paris, and there are limousines filled with the most stunning celebrities Hollywood and beyond have to offer.

They've closed down the whole of the New York Public Library for one day, an impossible feat for both kings and CEOs, but a single phone call from the goblin royal family, known to the world as entertainment-industry legends, achieves just that. Jett and her shambling crew of the undead have erected silken banners of rich, vibrant shades and created an entire custom lighting setup that bounces rays off the fabric and bathes the entire library in striking, kaleidoscopic color.

Jett is herding them all back into a large moving truck when Lena and Darren arrive with the catering vans to unload and set up all the food for the reception.

"No stragglers, people!" she shouts cordially, waving them up the ramp, speaking into the strange biological abscess attached to her ear that allows her to control their actions.

"All the finery rocking it, Jett?" Bronko asks, climbing out from behind the wheel of his vintage GTO Judge.

The two catering vans fall in behind it.

"It's a masterpiece, Byron. I will absolutely toot my own horn. The king and queen love it."

"What about the bride and groom?"

"Right. Yes. Them, too."

"Uh-huh." Bronko offers her a tiny pastry-wrapped lobster Wellington, one of several hundred in the vans behind him. "A job well done, my dear."

"Ooooh," Jett swoons, popping the appetizer into her mouth. "Divine, Byron. As always."

"Thank ya kindly."

The entire kitchen staff of Sin du Jour begins unloading the vans, half of them setting up the food inside while the other half cart tall steel towers slotted with trays full of their hard weeks of labor.

Nikki has already set up shop in a staging area through two large closed doors just off the main reception area. It is through those doors that the mountainous five-tiered replica cake will be wheeled and presented to the assemblage at the end of dinner.

Darren does his best to ignore the flashes of celebrity he catches moving in and out of the building and passing the corridors through which they're setting up for dinner.

He has less luck ignoring the uniformed guards stationed everywhere. They're not prototypical police or private security; they're all wearing ceremonial-looking uniforms with arcane symbols emblazoned on them Darren can't read.

They also all seem very familiar.

"Am I wrong or is, like, the cast from every show on the CW working security at this wedding?"

"Goblin hierarchy," Bronko explains. "Doesn't matter how hot or how famous they are in the rest of the world, they have to work their way up the ladder in goblin society just like everyone else. It's an honor to be wearing those monkey suits, serving as honor guard for a gig like this."

"That's crazy," Darren says, but he's smiling unbidden like a child.

"You're really digging all of this, aren't you?" Lena asks them as they wheel tray towers of appetizers inside.

"You're not?"

"I'm digging our rent being paid for the rest of the year," she states flatly.

When they return to the vans Bronko has Dorsky,

Rollo, and James corralled around him.

"And those two," they hear Bronko say as they approach.

"What's up, Chef?" Darren asks.

"You're coming with us back to the kitchen to get the rest of the food," Dorsky informs them.

"Why do we only have two vans?" Rollo asks bluntly. "We're government-funded on top of working for the most powerful people and nonpeople in the world. Why don't we have, like, air ships? Like in *Avengers*?"

Bronko looks to his sous-chef wearily.

"Shut up, Rollo," Dorsky says.

"Fine."

"Is there a reason the busboys aren't schlepping with us?" Lena asks.

Pacific, Mr. Mirabal, and a half-dozen other hires for the wedding are currently holding court at the bottom of the library steps, clandestinely passing a joint.

"It's not like they're risking life and limb for this one."

"I like to keep anyone working front of the house as calm as possible before service," Bronko explains. "Which we'll start while you cart the rest of the food over here. We should be good with the first load. I just want to make sure we're covered."

"On it, Chef," Dorsky assures him.

He motions to the rest and Rollo, James, Lena, and

Darren all pile back into the catering vans.

THE TOAST

Bianca's uncle Ted didn't wait.

The steel rainfall of metal tapping glass rang out just as the immaculately plated appetizers and salads were placed in front of the first tables.

Everyone else waited.

The best man waited for the general chatter to die down.

The guests waited for him to begin his toast.

Uncle Ted, on the other hand, was drunk and hungry and simply didn't give a fuck. He took up his fork and plowed into the food in front of him with the ferocity and efficiency of a marine in a mess hall.

The rest of his table ignored the breach of etiquette, raised their glasses in honor of the newly married royal couple, and then politely began enjoying their meal.

Uncle Ted is practically ready for dessert.

Meanwhile, Bronko has stepped outside the library to enjoy a cigar and await the arrival of his chefs and the excess plates.

He's just lighting the stogie with an old-fashioned

stick match when a rumbling draws his attention.

It's Jett's moving truck.

Bronko squints, waving the match to extinguish it.

He didn't realize the truck was still parked there, expecting Jett to have returned her crew to holding at Sin du Jour.

Instead it's rocking gently from side to side at the curb, no one behind the wheel, back closed up tight.

Bronko walks over to the truck's rear.

"Jett?" he calls around the stogie in his mouth. "You in there?"

A gentle panic begins to fill him as he pictures the excitable woman's undead minions somehow breaking their control and devouring her whole.

Bronko makes a grab for the truck's latch and throws the doors open.

The undead workers aren't rapt in a feeding frenzy.

They're all pressed against the walls of the truck, trembling as if confused or frightened or both.

Bronko squints into the darkness.

Something is moving very fast from side to side there.

That something abruptly springs from the shadows and launches itself at him.

Stogie still clutched between his teeth, Bronko finds one hand grasping Chanel while his other grips what feels like scales.

A giant, bipedal reptile wearing Jett's suit is attacking him, he realizes with only minor horror.

Actually, it's not attacking him, and that second realization spikes his horror significantly higher.

It's trying to hump him.

Is humping him, in fact.

It might be funny in the most inopportune way if it weren't accompanied by sharp claws and sharper fangs, both of which are snapping at him while Jett growls and grinds feverishly atop him.

"What the fuck!" he hollers, rearing back and hurling the Jett-creature away from him with all his might.

The horny reptilian being skitters across the pavement, righting itself quickly.

Bronko only has time to get to his knees before she/ it leaps at him anew.

Fortunately for Bronko the reptilian creature is every bit as petite as Jett. He overwhelms its size, and his strength allows him to wrestle it under control. Not wanting to toss it/her back into the moving truck with the undead, he drags the Jett-creature over to his Judge, pops the trunk with a mighty kick, and tosses her inside, closing the lid and sealing her in.

Somehow through it all he hasn't bitten through his stogie. His ragged, elevated breathing draws in smoke, and he coughs roughly around it.

Bronko removes the cigar from his mouth and casts it into the gutter.

His mind is reeling.

"Okay," he says to himself. "Okay . . . think now . . ."

And he does.

And the image of him handing Jett one of their wedding appetizers hit him.

And Bronko runs back into the library.

Or rather, he attempts to run back inside.

Five feet from the nearest entrance Bronko runs smack into an invisible field of energy as solid and impassable as steel.

It knocks him onto the pavement for a third time.

"Fuck me!" he yells, and it's not in pain or confusion.

He knows exactly what's happening.

BRICK DOORS, BRICK WINDOWS

The boys are lounging in the main kitchen, sitting among the final tray towers laughing and indulging in shots of Jameson provided by Dorsky, whose taken one of the vans down to the corner to get gas.

They're also indulging in a few appetizers.

Lena has left them to it. On the way over she received a call from Nikki on her cell, asking Lena to grab her purse, which she left behind.

Lena is walking back from the pastry kitchen when she hears the first rumblings, the first gnashing of inhuman teeth and grotesque sounds of moist friction.

She halts, puzzling at it.

She also spots Dorsky at the other end of the hall, walking from the lobby entrance to the building.

He pauses as he hears it too.

They trade puzzled looks from afar, neither of them speaking aloud.

Eventually their feet begin carrying them forward again.

They meet at the archway leading into the main

kitchen.

They both peer inside at the same time.

Processing that for which you have no frame of reference is always the most difficult thing for the human mind to do.

Neither Lena nor Dorsky has a frame of reference for watching a trio of giant lizard-men wearing Sin du Jour smocks savagely fucking each other in their kitchen.

But that's exactly what they're looking at.

Lena is horrified beyond responding.

Dorsky is at least able to grasp the situation at some base, instinctual level.

This is his kitchen, and these things are destroying it.

"Hey!" he yells angrily. "What the fuck is this?"

Lena shoots him an equally horrified look.

Her own instincts tell her that drawing the attention of these things is a mistake.

Her instincts are correct.

In the next moment they are both booking it for the lobby as the fornicating snake people disengage and tear after them, snarling and growling ferociously.

Lena is faster on her feet. She hits the lobby first.

Dorsky isn't far behind, but he stops just past the entrance from the hall to the lobby and throws closed the two plywood doors that usually stand open at all times.

There's no lock on them, but there are two vending

machines in the lobby.

The reptilian creatures hit the doors from the other side a second after Dorsky topples the first steel-and-glass kiosk in front of them. It's enough to halt them momentarily, and enough time for him to heave over the second vending machine. It lands on the first, shattering and spilling off-brand candy all over the floor.

Dorsky turns, expecting Lena to be in the street by now.

She's not.

Instead she's standing in front of what used to be the entrance to Sin du Jour.

Both of her hands are pushing against a solid wall of brick that has suddenly, miraculously replaced those glass doors.

"Oh, shit," is all Dorsky manages.

NO RECEPTION

Nikki is dabbing at one of several hundred plates with perfectly symmetrical cake pieces resting on them when she hears the commotion in the reception area.

She looks up, and Pacific and Mr. Mirabel are peeking through the two huge reveal doors.

"What's going on?" she asks.

"This giant lizard thing in a tux is trying to bone that dude from *Grey's Anatomy*," Pacific says, totally unfazed. "You know, the one with the hair."

It's so outrageous and so patently Pacific that Nikki dismisses it outright.

"I really wish you guys would wait to smoke that shit until after work," she says, returning her attention to her plates.

"No, seriously," Pacific says.

"For real, mami," Mr. Mirabal adds, much more in awe of whatever he's looking at through the door.

Brow furrowed, Nikki drops her cloth and skitters over to the doors, nudging them both aside and peering through the crack.

And sees a giant lizard thing in a tux trying to hump the guy from *Grey's Anatomy* with the hair.

"Oh, my god," she gasps.

"Yeah."

"Sí."

The uniformed goblin honor guard is trying to wrestle a drunk, reptilian, lust-possessed Uncle Ted off of the famous film and television actor.

They're not doing a very good job of it, either.

Nikki, transfixed, can't help slipping through the doors and wandering toward the epicenter of the strange atrocity.

More of the honor guard and a few NBA players are now trying to help wrangle the Uncle Ted–creature under control.

"Everyone be calm!" the goblin king booms above the frightened and shocked gasps and chatter.

Reinforced, they manage to pull the giant, sex-crazed reptile off of the actor and wrestle him/it to the floor.

The situation is finally settling down when virtually every single human guest at the reception begins to change.

Some scream, some yell, some throw themselves to the floor.

But they all begin to transform.

It is, in a word, unsettling.

Flesh stretches and mangles itself and changes into seven sickly shades of yellow and green.

Scales and fins and other new, frightening appendages shred through tuxedos and gowns.

Human cries of panic and pain become hideous animalistic shrieks of desire.

It's a nightmare.

And then the nightmare becomes a porno.

The creatures tear into each other, violently, but theirs is a lust-born violence, and the end result is hundreds of bipedal reptiles having an orgy in the middle of the New York Public Library.

And the ones who don't immediately seek a partner of their own kind go after the goblins.

There's a new round of panicked shrieks as celebrities bat at the creatures and attempt to flee.

Nikki also turns to flee back into the staging area.

She never sees the Oscar-winning actress who also does those glossy makeup commercials wildly swinging a bottle of nine-hundred-dollar champagne.

But her skull does feel the impact.

The rest is blessed darkness and equally blessed silence.

NOTHIN' BUT A HOUND DOG

Lena pounds her fists against the sudden brick.

It's as real as it appears to be.

With a frustrated yell, she steps back and turns to face Dorsky.

The lobby is dark now, despite the waning sun still hanging high over the brick building. The windows facing the street have also become patches of solid brick. The interior windows looking out onto the stone courtyard in the center of the complex haven't been mystically bricked over, but the piece of the roof opening down onto the courtyard has.

"What the fuck is happening?" she yells over the cacophony of howling, psychotically amorous reptiles trying to break through the vending machine–reinforced lobby doors.

Dorsky only manages a bewildered, panicked half-shrug.

"I'm afraid the entire building has been sealed off, ma'am," a pinched, nasal monotone voice informs them.

Both of them turn their heads and look down.

Standing in the center of the lobby is a three-foot-tall animated hound dog.

It's a cartoon.

A three-dimensional, living cartoon.

Both Lena and Dorsky stare down at its drooping features. It's wearing a collar with a wordless gold tag and its half-lidded, weary eyes seem to stare through them rather than at them.

"You . . . what?" Lena snaps at the image.

"Please be more specific with your question, ma'am."

"What the hell is happening?" Lena says desperately, not really addressing the cartoon hound, but speaking in general helplessness.

"As I said, ma'am. An emergency enchantment has been activated by the detection of unauthorized level-nine magical creatures on the premises. The building has been completely sealed to prevent anyone or anything from exiting."

Dorsky looks back at the vending machines propped against the lobby doors, the hinges of which are beginning to buckle under the force of the battering from the other side.

"Which means . . ."

"You're trapped here, sir," the toon informs him.

PART III

LOCKDOWN

THE OUTSIDERS

Ryland walks right into the patch of solid brick where Sin du Jour's service entrance used to be before he notices there's no longer a door there.

He'd just reached that point he often hits at fourteen hours of constant wine consumption, when he realizes if he doesn't eat something he'll begin vomiting liquid followed by a dry maelstrom of heaving. Emerging from his booted, disused RV forever parked behind Sin du Jour, half-smoked cigarette between two right fingers that also helped support a rapidly diminished glass of white wine, Ryland made the forty-seven-step trek to the back door.

He was mumbling something about spinach puffs when his nose dimly registered the pain of a sudden collision.

Now he's staring blearily at the red brick, the slow rudders of his mind trying to steer the information toward some manner of recognition.

He reaches out with his free hand and tests the solidity of the barrier.

It holds.

This new piece of information helps drive home his initial encounter with the brick.

"Well," he muses aloud. "That is certainly an odd thing that's happening there."

Ryland copes with the oddity of the situation by draining the remainder of his wineglass.

Staring into the golden residue of the glass's otherwise empty bottom, Ryland thinks to himself that this is the moment a person with a mobile phone would utilize such an instrument.

Unfortunately he's never owned one and doesn't intend to remedy that.

So instead he retreats to one of the bird-eaten lawn chairs in front of his RV, reclines awkwardly on it, and pours himself another glass of wine from a nearby bottle.

He does, however, stare intently at the door as he drinks.

He's still staring and drinking a half-hour later when Ritter comes bounding around the north side of the large brick-and-mortar edifice.

"It's useless," Ryland assures him from around his next cigarette as Ritter rushes past.

He watches the head of Sin du Jour's stocking and receiving department push against the transformed entrance briefly and then back away from it, fists jammed against his hips.

"The main ingress is the same, I expect?" Ryland asks him.

"Yeah," Ritter answers without turning around. "It's a security enchantment. The building locks itself down when it detects a nonhuman threat."

"Yes, well, that makes sense in a sort of lateral way, I suppose. Would you care for a drink?"

Ritter finally turns from the nondoor and walks over to him.

"Who's in there right now?"

"Uh . . . Dorsky and a few of the cooks. The partially demonic sea hag. The elderly Navajo and his tauntingly attractive daughter. Oh, the new girl with the perpetually severe expression on her face—"

"Lena?"

"If you say so."

Ritter stares back at the bricked-up entrance with renewed urgency in his eyes.

Even Ryland isn't that oblivious.

"Are you and she carrying on something sordid, then? That was fast."

Ritter ignores the question and the comment.

He takes out his phone and sends a group text to Cindy, Hara, and Moon.

It's a simple message: "Code Red."

As he types and sends: "Is it the booze that makes

you this useless, Ryland, or is that just how you live with it?"

Ryland shrugs, thoroughly uninsulted.

"You'd have to ask me when I'm sober, I imagine."

Ritter nods, lowering his phone and staring back at the sealed-off building.

"I won't hold my breath or anything."

SATURDAY MORNING CARTOONS

"It's Droopy Hound," Dorsky says.

Lena looks up at him, then back at the living animation cell. "What?"

"From . . . the Banjo Bear Gang. You know. The cartoons. From back in the . . . day."

Behind them a dripping talon breaks off the entire corner of one of the hallway doors.

"No way that holds," Dorsky observes.

"What the hell are you?" Lena asks Droopy Hound.

"I'm bound to the enchantment protecting your domicile, ma'am. I'm its keeper."

"What happened to my line?" Dorsky asks. "What are those things?"

"They appear to have been transformed by a rare magical herb, ma'am."

"Into what?"

"Manifestations of pure lust."

"What the hell does that mean?"

"So you're saying they don't want to kill us, they want to fuck us?"

"At that level of desire the two acts are interchangeable, sir."

"Great. So if they break through that shit they're going to fuck us to death?"

"Precisely, sir."

"Can you let us out of here?" Lena asks.

"Of course I can, ma'am."

They wait.

"Well?" Lena demands. "Let us out of here!"

The droopy hound continues to stare passively through them.

"What's wrong with you? You're supposed to protect us! Let us the fuck out!"

"No, ma'am."

"Why not?"

That's when Droopy Hound's eyes focus on them for the first time, intently. The toon smiles wide, and the abrupt change in such a classically mopey face makes the cartoon look suddenly, utterly terrifying.

"The spell binding me prescribes only that I keep anyone or anything from leaving the premises and forbids me from doing those premises and their natural occupants harm, ma'am. And I've been trapped in this security enchantment for a long time. I'm quite eager for entertainment. I'll find your blood and guts most entertaining, I think. Yes, it's been a very long time."

Dorsky's body becomes a cocktail of rage and shock. "What kind of fucking cartoon character are you, man?"

Lena thrusts a hand into his chest to silence him.

"Is there a way for *us* to stop them from getting to us? Can you at least tell us that?" A thought occurs to her, and she adds desperately, "It'll make it more . . . whatever . . . sporting!"

The droopy hound hesitates.

"Yes," he finally says, more relenting than affirming.

It's his hesitation more than his tone that gives Lena pause.

"Will you tell us?" she asks tentatively.

"No," he says, without hesitation this time.

Dorsky looks at her quizzically.

"What—"

She shakes her head, speaking over him. "Do you have to answer our questions? Is that part of this . . . program . . . enchantment . . . whatever?"

"Yes," the droopy hound says, his already deflated voice sounding particularly defeated now.

"So you don't have to let us out, but you have to give us information if we ask?"

"Yes."

She points back at the rapidly failing barricade. "How do we stop them from breaking through that?"

"There are emergency measures embedded in the reception kiosk, ma'am."

Lena and Dorsky both look over at the empty reception area.

"I always wondered why the hell that thing is there," Dorsky says. "We haven't had a secretary since I've been here."

"Receptionist," Lena corrects him before making a beeline for the desk.

Dorsky follows.

She leaps over the front of the tall crescent and stands over the empty desktop. "Where are they?" Lena asks Droopy Hound. "How do we use them?"

With both a literally and figuratively animated sigh the hound waves one of his anthropomorphic canine hands.

Before Lena a map of the entire building's interior appears.

"Simply touch the area you wish to secure," Droopy Hound instructs her.

Lena moves her finger over the map, locating the lobby.

She taps the archway between reception and the main hall.

Both she and Dorksy look to the steadily faltering plywood doors with their vending machine reinforcements.

The plywood instantly becomes the same solid brick filling all the exterior passages.

They both breathe a little easier.

"All right, now how do we change them back?" Lena immediately asks the droopy hound.

"There's an herbal remedy in a small room of the east wing."

"Boosha," they say practically in unison.

"How do we get—" Dorsky begins.

"We'll go through the courtyard," Lena says, already picking up a heavy chair.

"Wait. What if—"

The next sound is the window behind the reception desk shattering.

Lena steps in front of it and begins chipping away the jagged teeth left in the bottom of the window frame with her sleeve-covered hand.

Dorsky watches her.

"Not for nothing, but this is the second time this window's been broken since you showed up. Not to mention this is the second gig we've done to go fucking haywire."

"So it's my fault?"

Drosky shrugs.

"You are such a dick," she says, climbing through the window.

"That's me," he mutters after her. "Dicksy, sous-chef

to the stars."

"You're both going to die here, you know," the dreary, nasal voice assures him.

Dorsky turns from the window to see Droopy Hound standing directly beneath him.

The toon's normally passive eyes are now burning red and staring directly up at him.

Then the animated character fizzles and blinks out, as if someone has just changed the channel on an old television set.

HOLLOW VISITATION

"You blowing the smoke in her face, man."

"Oh, my bad."

The voices draw Nikki back to the waking world. The lights sting her fluttering eyes and it takes her several moments to adjust. She also smells acrid, slightly sweet smoke. When the vague shapes in her field of vision clarify themselves she finds she's staring up at the concerned-yet-somehow-still-chill faces of Pacific and Mr. Mirabal as they lean over her prone form. Nikki quickly realizes she's lying on the first immaculate tier of the thirty-foot pearl-and-diamond-crusted faux cake she helped design for the goblin prince's wedding.

It's horrifically uncomfortable.

"What . . . happened?"

"Like, half the guest list turned into these trippy reptilian things and they all started humping each other. It was some serious Hunter S. Thompson *Fear and Loathing*–type shit."

"Then they all come after us," Mr. Mirabal adds.

"Yeah, Mo here had to crack Uncle Ted with his oxy

tank to keep him from going all frat boy on you while you were out. It was not cool. But no one's dead. Pretty sure, anyway. Most of the goblin celebs climbed up the stacks in the back of the library."

Nikki sits up slowly, a small battalion riding unshod between her temples. She winces, but forces her eyes to stay open and scan the room.

They're barricaded in the staging area. Shipping containers and kitchen equipment, and several large pieces of furniture, block the large doors through which the cake was to be rolled out and presented.

Across the room Prince Marek and Bianca (now Princess Bianca, Nikki thinks to herself) are kneeling over the carefully laid out bodies of the goblin king and queen.

"Oh, my god. What about Davi—. . . what about the king and queen?"

Pacific waves it off. "Oh, they're cool. They just got dropped hard the same way you did herding the other—you know—nonmonstery guests back here."

Nikki nods. "Can we get out through the windows?"

"Negative," Pac says in the strained wake of a long toke on his joint. "There's some kind of gnarly mystic field around the whole building."

"What?"

"Yeah, we figure it's some kind of emergency-type

deal in case . . . well, shit like this happens. One of those things tried to take a powder outside after they all turned."

"Smack right into it," Mr. Mirabal informs her, driving a fist into the palm of his opposite hand.

"So at least they can't get out. But neither can we, so." Pacific shrugs.

"Then someone will be coming for us, right?" Nikki asks. "To help us?"

"Help will not come," a matronly voice somehow speaking right beside Mr. Mirabal assures them.

They all turn to see Boosha standing in their midst.

"Boosh!" Pac exclaims, almost laughing. "You're like a ninja, man. How did you get in here?"

"I am not here," the ancient woman informs them. "I am back in my kitchen. What is happening here is happening there."

Pacific's brow furrows. "Wait . . . you mean . . . what's happening here, like where you actually are . . . or 'here' as in, like, where your body actually is?"

"Same thing!" Boosha snaps.

"Right. Sorry. So you're, like, astral whatever?"

Pacific reaches out and passes a hand through Boosha's illusory form.

"Swirly," he says.

"Boosha, what the heck is happening?" Nikki asks.

The old woman looks more pensive and hesitant than Nikki has ever seen her, or at least the projection of Boosha does.

"Fault is mine," she says. "I sprinkle human food with herbs by accident . . . meant for goblins . . . powerful love spell, to make everyone happy. In humans it is too strong . . . turns them into creatures of pure lust."

Pacific nods. "Literally."

"Hold on!"

It's Prince Marek.

"Are you saying you people did this?" he demands. "You're responsible for what's happened to everyone in the whole world my wife knows or cares about?"

"Was mistake!" Boosha snaps, then holds up a finger and shakes it violently at Marek. "Mistake not happen if prince's family not treat lovely human girl and family like outcast, like . . . like . . . less!"

"What . . ." Marek looks from the image of Boosha to his new bride.

"I didn't ask for this, Marek," Bianca says.

"She did not. As I said, is my mistake."

"Boosha," Nikki cuts in. "What do you mean no one is coming? What about Mister Allensworth and his people?"

She shrugs. "All they care is that these things are contained. They will wait, see how they work themselves out.

Is their way."

"Your people are just going to trap us in here and leave us to die?"

"Is price you all pay for fame and fortune of human world!" Boosha thunders right back at them.

Nikki shouts over them all: "Then how do *we* change the guests back, Boosha? Can we even do that?"

Boosha's lips purse. "Herbs to reverse spell are here, with me. However . . . you have what you need in food there to make . . . what is word? Temporary? You make temporary cure. I show you. Make dust. Dust goes in face of lust creatures. Dust is absorbed through eyes and nose and mouth. Results should come quickly."

"Sweet," Pacific says. "So all we have to do is walk back out there and ask the horny monsters to line up so we can dust them in the face. You know, without them gangbanging us in half and all."

Mr. Mirabal shakes his head, inhaling deeply through the oxygen tube stretched beneath his nostrils. "No way, man. No way."

Nikki, on the other hand, has moved directly past doubt and fear. She's staring up the length of the massive decorative cake, a look of pure steel on her face.

Around the kitchen of Sin du Jour this is known as Nikki's "get it done" look.

It is never to be trifled with.

Nikki looks from the top of the cake to her ravaged baking station, more specifically at the large piping bags strewn about the counter and floor.

"Okay, then," she says simply.

"If we're truly on our own here," Prince Marek says, "then anything that's to be done we'll do together."

"All of us," Bianca adds firmly.

Her prince seems taken aback for a moment, but then nods resolutely, reaching out and taking her hand.

Nikki watches them, and at that moment, amid the madness and anger and tension and peril, the two seem to coalesce together, becoming a unit.

She smiles, all but forgetting the desperate plan she's just formulated that may result in all of their violent deaths.

"Do you two want to at least have a piece of your own wedding cake first?" she asks them.

I CAME TO MAKE A BANG, YEAH

Cindy adheres the final liner strip to the center of the bricked-in entrance behind Sin du Jour.

As she does, Ritter continues tapping a simple message in Morse code against the brick with the spike of Cindy's tactical tomahawk, advising anyone on the other side to back away and take cover.

Moon cocks his head, watching them from a safe distance. "So is this, like, dynamite?"

"It's HMX compounded with three percent polymer-bonded explosive composite," Cindy says around the grip of the diagonal pliers clinched between her teeth.

"Did you say that all extra technical to make me feel like an asshole?" Moon asks.

"Mm-hmmm."

Several seconds pass and Cindy steps back from her handiwork, removing the pliers from her mouth.

"All right," she says to Ritter. "We're hot. I've shaped the charge to minimize the scattering of debris when it blows, but I don't know how physical objects will react under whatever enchantment this is."

He nods, turning and motioning to Moon to take refuge behind the RV.

As Ritter jogs after him, Cindy retreats behind the explosive shield she's bolted to the ground the minimum safe distance from the entrance. She's holding the detonator in her gloved left hand.

"We're lighting it up in five!" she calls out.

Ryland, refusing to vacate his lawn chair, empties his wineglass in a single, frantic gulp and then sticks a fingertip in each ear, still holding his cigarette.

Cindy cups her hands around the detonator, lowering her chin against her chest.

"Five . . . four . . . three . . ."

Two seconds later she clamps her hands tight around the detonator, then releases it and repeats the action.

The sound of the blast is little more than a typhoid cough when it reaches the street, but in the immediate vicinity of the service entrance it's enough to set ears ringing and shatter the wineglass in Ryland's hand.

The rear of the building is covered in a veil of white smoke, and redbrick dust fills the alley, clinging to the exposed skin and clothes of everyone in it.

"What was that bullshit about 'minimizing' or whatever?" Moon calls out, hacking on the dust as he and Ritter emerge from behind the RV.

Cindy ignores him, moving from behind the blast

shield and waving her way through the dust and smoke.

Ryland gropes for his white wine bottle, wiping its mouth with his shirt (which is far more soiled than the mouth of the bottle itself) and drinking directly from it.

"Truly, I have achieved the American dream," he mumbles drunkenly.

"Cindy?" Ritter calls through the haze.

"Son of a bitch!" she screams.

They all hack on the debris for another thirty seconds until enough of it has been swept down the alley to see the rear of the building clearly again.

Despite the red cloud raised by the blast, the bricked-over service entrance appears completely undisturbed.

There isn't a visible scratch on it.

Cindy unhooks the tomahawk strapped to her right leg and chops at the center of the brick patch with its blade, just to be sure.

Solid as brick and mortar.

At that moment gas-powered thunder fills the alley and a monstrous motorcycle twice the size of any other commercial bike rolls beside Ryland's RV. Its rider is almost perfectly proportioned atop the massive vehicle.

It's the only time Hara ever looks relatively normal in size.

He pulls off a helmet the size of a witch's cauldron and climbs from the massive Leonhardt Gunbus. He takes in the scene for several long moments, then looks to Ritter, perpetually silent and questioning with his expression.

"Someone fill him in while I think of what the hell to try next," Ritter says with more exasperation than they've ever heard in his voice.

They all watch as he climbs the steps into Ryland's trailer and closes the door behind him.

"Grab me another glass, will you?" Ryland calls after him.

THE OBSTINANCE OF ANCESTORS

The six-foot reptile wearing what's left of Darren's formerly fresh and fitted Sin du Jour smock is suspended three feet off the ground over an elaborate sand painting.

The lustful creature snarls and thrashes against its invisible bonds, but whatever force has bound it there in midair holds tight.

Orbiting the creature in staggered spirals, small wisps of milky white energy undulate and pass through one another, creating cymbal crashes of sound and bursts of light each time they harmlessly collide.

Little Dove takes in the sight from the corner of the sand painting, arms folded and brow furrowed.

She looks down at her grandfather, seated cross-legged in front of the large square frame holding the sand. He chants absently as he hand-rolls a cigarette he's laced with weed stolen from one of Pacific's many stashes around the building.

"So . . . these are our ancestors?" Little Dove asks the old man. "Their spirits, anyway?"

White Horse nods, sealing the tightly rolled wrapping paper with an envelope lick of his tongue.

"Yep."

Little Dove is dubious. "For real?"

"Yep," he says, perching the cigarette on his bottom lip. He motions to one of the white wisps with one hand while the other searches his elk-skin jacket for his lighter. "That there is your great-grandfather, Long Knife. And that other one there is Aunt Margaret. And that there is your third cousin, Lloyd."

She rolls her eyes. "You're so fucking with me right now."

"Yep."

Little Dove curses under her breath while her grandfather, having located his light, sparks it and burns the end of his cigarette, drawing the smoke deep into his lungs.

He coughs, with immense relish.

The door to their offices stands wide open.

When the chaos erupted, rather than barricading themselves inside White Horse simply moved his sand painting board in front of the door and set to work on a design his granddaughter had never seen before.

Darren was the first creature to sniff them out, and as soon as he rushed inside he was caught, rapt.

It's been more than enough to ward off the other creatures their coworkers have become.

"They are the spirit of your ancestors," he says seriously. "But you have to think of it as a pond of energy to which we all return. There's no discerning or separating. Their energy protects us when called upon. We're connected, by blood and by our spirits. It's their instinct. It's really not complicated."

"Yeah, I'm sure I can just Google it."

"Probably."

Little Dove paces in front of the sand painting, watching the Darren-creature flare its nostrils in frustration.

"So can you change him back?"

White Horse exhales a long trail of smoke and leans back against the floor, propped up by his elbows.

"It wasn't my power that did this to him, or the rest."

Little Dove stops pacing and glares down at him. "That's not what I asked, Pop. Can you fix him?"

"Probably."

"Then do it!"

White Horse frowns. "They pay me to help conjure and cleanse their crazy bilagáana food. They don't pay me to clean up their messes. We're safe back here. Let the rest of them figure it out."

"'Them'?" Little Dove hisses at him angrily. "You mean like Bronko? That awesome guy who got us off the res? Who paid for us to move to New York City? Who paid off all of Papa's debt?"

"They've been making a mess of this land for four hundred years," White Horse mutters grouchily.

"Oh, Pop, spare me the Ken Burns documentary, all right? They're not the fucking Union cavalry. They're the people we work with every day." She motions back at the Darren-creature. "This kid's been here, like, a month, he doesn't know what the hell he's even in for yet. If you can fix him, then do it already."

The old man sucks on his cigarette and grumbles to himself for another full thirty seconds, looking anywhere but at her.

Then he reluctantly climbs to his feet.

"Stand against the wall," he instructs her.

Little Dove nods, moving to the far wall and leaning back against it.

White Horse stubs out his carefully fashioned cigarette on the hard sole of his boot, brushing off the end and slipping it into one of his jacket pockets.

He walks over to the desk and opens a drawer, removing a small sprig of green herbs.

"Is that sage?" she asks him.

"No, it's oregano from the kitchen, but it doesn't really matter."

White Horse stands in front of the sand painting and lights the herbs ablaze.

He spreads his arms out wide before the Darren-creature who, sensing danger, begins thrashing anew.

"What are you going to do?"

"His spirit contains his true self," White Horse explains impatiently. "It can overcome the magic holding his form in thrall. I'm going to call to that spirit, wake it from its slumber. Now shut the hell up, will you?"

Little Dove mimes zipping her lip.

She also uses her middle finger to do so.

The old man begins chanting in earnest, his normally ragged, noncommittal voice becoming impossibly deep and powerful. He taunts the Darren-creature with the burning herbs. The wisps of energy circling him begin to move faster, more erratically, somehow taking on an air of menace.

Little Dove feels the barometric pressure in the room change abruptly. She hugs herself against it, watching as the lights begin to flicker.

The creature held suspended there is no longer thrashing. It now appears that a separate force is moving its reptilian form, shaking it fiercely.

White Horse's chanting voice becomes almost godlike in its power and fury.

His granddaughter finds herself shrinking against the wall in sudden, confused fear.

The lust creature becomes a blur of motion.

The chanting reaches a thunderous crescendo.

Then it all stops.

A half-naked, sweat-soaked Darren falls on his hands and knees against the sand, gulping desperately for air.

Little Dove slides back up the wall.

She steps tentatively to the middle of the room.

"Are you . . . okay?" she asks Darren.

"He's fine," White Horse insists.

The old man is doubled over, hands clasping his knees.

He's also panting.

"Get me some water, will you?" he asks her.

Little Dove nods, running to grab a bottle of designer water from their miniature fridge. She also grabs an emergency blanket for Darren.

Thrusting the water roughly into White Horse's chest as he stands, Little Dove spreads the blanket over Darren.

He finally raises his head, his eyes wide and tear-filled and mystified.

"What . . . I . . ."

"Shhhhhh," she coos to him, stroking his damp hair. "Don't try to talk or . . . you know, move around a lot for a little bit, okay? You were just a really big snake thing."

Darren stares up at her, somehow even more confused now.

Little Dove shakes her head, silently cursing herself. "Just . . . never mind right now."

She looks up at her grandfather. "Okay, now fix the rest of them. Then maybe the doors and windows will change back."

White Horse stares at her.

Her expression only hardens further.

"You change them all back or I swear to God you can take care of yourself from now on."

He frowns deeply, sighing. "I swear, you are worse than all three of my wives put together, including your grandma."

Little Dove turns back to Darren, mostly to conceal her grin.

White Horse pats himself down, searching frantically for his cigarette before adding with vigor: "And she was the worst one!"

99 PROBLEMS AND A BRICK IS ONE

"I guess the only thing left to do is have Moon eat his way through the fucking thing," Cindy says without even attempting to mask the defeat in her voice.

"I'm not a carnie, you know," he snipes back.

Ritter ignores them both, surveying the wreckage of the past few hours and their failed attempts to breach the magical barriers of Sin du Jour.

Hara's customary stoic posture and expression make him resemble a brick statue now that he's antiqued in red dust. The industrial jackhammer none of the rest of them could even lift has been discarded on the ground beside him, its bit worn to a twisted steel nub. Every grain he pounded from the entrance replicated itself immediately.

Ryland is now splayed over his lawn chair upside down, staring up at the waning sun as if it is some unmerciful god. The cigarette perched on his lips bobs animatedly as he mutters inaudibly to himself. He's caked head to toe in dried white froth. His attempt to change the brick into a soft custard through which they might dig did not, needless to say, end well.

"No," Ritter says to Cindy, a dangerous steel coming to his voice. "It's my turn."

Before she can ask what the hell that means Ritter begins stripping his clothes off.

He's down to his waist when Bronko's Judge pulls into the alley with what sounds like a marching band on meth inside his trunk.

After he parks and climbs out of the vintage car it takes Bronko less than ten seconds to assess the situation.

"Goddamn muckraking fuckbudget," is how he summarizes things.

"The wedding gig?" Ritter asks.

Bronko nods. "Locked down. It's the food. I don't know. But I know what it's doing to 'em."

He looks back at the dented-out trunk of his car.

The rest of them are already staring at it.

"You got one of ours in there?" Ritter asks.

Bronko sighs. "I hope she still is, yeah."

CONTROL OF THE SITUATION

"You sure as shit looked like you knew where you were going."

"I've been here a month, asshole! You've been here for years!"

"And if I'd pointed that out you would've had some smartass reason it didn't matter!"

They're back in the Sin du Jour courtyard. The second window Lena smashed (this time using Pacific's beloved patio chair) led them into a wing of the building that can only access the corridor leading to Boosha's apothecary through an exterior door. Which, of course, is now made entirely of brick.

"That shouldn't have stopped you!" Lena shoots back at Dorsky, marching several feet ahead of him.

A sharp electric buzz precedes the living cartoon materializing in front of them.

It's Droopy Hound.

This time, however, he's wearing a chef's smock and floppy toque on his head.

"I told you, folks," he says in his passive, nasally monotone. "You won't be leaving this place alive. I am enjoying your scurrying, however."

Lena immediately picks up a rock from the courtyard floor and, growling with teeth bared, hurls it through the illusory being.

Its animated form doesn't stop the rock, but its passing through does disperse the toon in a hail of colored pixels.

"Why cartoons?" Dorsky asks, helplessly. "Why a fucking cartoon?"

"I don't know."

"You had a map," Dorsky points out. "You were standing in front of a map of the whole building. A goddamn enchanted map with control over all of the inside doors."

Lena spins on him, advancing with her finger forward as if it were the blade of a knife.

Dorsky actually backs up.

"This place is a maze! It's like four asylums smashed together! I'm surprised anyone finds their way out on a normal day, let alone when the place is sealed up by a magic fucking spell and filled with monsters, one of which is my goddamn roommate!"

"All I'm saying is you need to slow down and stop trying to control a situation that's clearly way the hell beyond your control."

"No one made you follow me," she says with finality.

"Yeah, well. I saw a nice ass and I followed it. That's just how I'm built, I guess."

All of the anger abruptly leaves Lena, and in its place is an all-consuming weariness.

She shakes her head.

"What?" Dorsky says, confused and almost alarmed by her sudden change in demeanor.

"You know . . . you were still an asshole, but you'd actually almost become a human being. And in one sentence you manage to take a good long piss all over that. Basic-ass line chef dude bullshit. I guess I shouldn't be surprised."

And that hits Dorsky harder and cuts him deeper than any insult or curse.

He knows how to be hated, even thrives on it.

He doesn't know how to deal with so clearly and starkly disappointing someone.

Lena sees it, subtle as his reaction is. She sees it and wonders if the guy she's been running for her life alongside isn't the false front. She wonders if the misogynistic asshole Dorsky tries so hard to be is the façade, one he adopted coming up through the ranks as so many of them do.

Unfortunately there's no time to sort through these complex interpersonal issues, because that's when a window across the courtyard shatters and a lustful creature twice the size of any of the others they saw in the kitchen leaps down upon the cobbles.

"Shit," Dorsky says as he takes in the size of it. "That's gotta be Rollo."

"It's kind of an improvement."

"Good. You fuck him. I'll run."

But they both run, turning and running in the same direction by chance more than anything else. Dorsky snatches up a dead potted plant on the run and hurls it through the nearest window. It's elevated like the rest, and without missing a beat he slides across the dirt-covered courtyard floor on his knees, cutting them on broken glass and halting just under the eave.

He cups his hands and offers a boost to Lena, who steps onto them and hoists herself up, chipping away the glass shards protruding from the bottom of the window frame with her elbow. She hoists herself through, ignoring the half-dozen tiny cuts she receives, and immediately leans back out to help Dorsky climb after her.

They end up in a disused prewar corridor in the west wing of the building.

"There!" Dorsky shouts, pointing at a heavy steel door half-open a few yards up the hallway.

They can hear the Rollo-creature taking half the window frame apart as it claws its way back into the building, but their backs are already turned and disappearing up the corridor.

Three cartoon puppies materialize in front of them. They're toddler versions of Droopy Hound, stacked on each other's shoulders, forming a living totem pole. Each is idly strumming a miniature string instrument.

"Your-blood-will-paint-the-walls," they sing-song in slow, droll unison. "Your-blood-will-paint-the-walls!"

Dorsky charges right through them without stopping, dispersing the cruel, ironic image.

He makes it to the door first, pulling it open and shoving his body through the crack at the same time. He reaches out and pulls an already sprinting Lena inside by the front of her smock.

They both slam the door shut behind them.

They're in an impossibly narrow closet with a single, petrified mop leaning against one corner.

There's no light.

Lena can feel her nose touching Dorsky's chest, heaving with his labored breathing. She can feel that breath against her hair.

He reaches up instinctually and lightly grasps her shoulders. Lena immediately and more indignantly than anything else shakes him off.

Those are her instincts.

Rollo is throwing his reptilian body against the other side of the door over and over again, snarling loudly and wantonly.

Fortunately the door was fashioned at a time before the American manufacturing industry's watchword became "disposable."

It's strong.

It holds.

Eventually the Rollo-creature's barrage ceases, although they can hear it growling and stalking just outside the door.

"Well," Dorsky whispers in the dark. "We're really fucked now."

"Pretty much."

"You don't sound overly concerned."

"I've been under fire before."

"Worse than this?"

"Different."

"What was it like?"

"Scary the first time. Really fucking scary."

"Of course. And the second time?"

"Still scary. But also . . . oddly comforting."

"Comforting how?"

" . . . I'd accepted the possibility of my own death, I guess. In a real way. Not in a bullshit, telling yourself you're ready for what comes way."

"So you were ready to die?"

"I was ready for it to be my choice. Fight or die. It felt

simple. Clean. It wasn't clean, obviously. Nothing over there was, but . . . in those moments. I don't know."

"And this? Here?"

"I mean, I'd rather not be fucked to death by a giant goddamn lizard, obviously."

"Obviously."

They share something that's almost but not quite laughter.

Neither of them speaks for a while after that.

The snarling and heavy pacing outside has dissipated.

They can feel the heat from each other's body, intensely. It should be unbearable there in such close quarters, but somehow they both find it comforting in that moment.

Dorsky's hands find her shoulders again.

This time Lena doesn't shake him off.

"If we're going to die here," Dorsky whispers into her hair, "I have two things I want to say to you."

"Fine."

"I'm sorry."

She looks up at him, not really able to make out his features in the dark, but somehow able to read his face.

He means it.

"Okay," she says evenly, or tries to. "What's the second thing, then?"

Dorsky presses her against the wall and kisses her lips.

There's surprise, and a fleeting montage in her head of every dick thing he's said and done to her and Darren since they showed up at Sin du Jour.

But there's also that heat, and his hands moving confidently and strongly over her body.

And the fact that he's discovered the one instance in life during which Lena does not want to be firmly in control of the situation.

She kisses him back, fiercely, her hands reaching up and tangling hard in his sweat-dampened hair.

She tells the little voice insisting that this is a mistake she'll regret later to shut the fuck up.

There may not be later.

By the time Dorsky rips open her smock Lena can no longer hear the little voice.

For the next twenty minutes she doesn't think about anything, not the peril or her choices or the lethal monstrosities awaiting them outside this dark cloister they've found, anything except the tactile pleasure of her own body.

And despite all of the evidence to the contrary, Dorsky is shockingly committed to that pleasure.

The sounds with which they fill that tiny closet are as raw and animal and unbound as any guttural cry made by the creatures of pure lust that have besieged the building.

Those cries build for each of them to their own deep,

brain-and-body-pulverizing crescendo.

Then they're quiet save for ragged, staccato breaths.

Then, somehow, they do it all over again.

Lena loses all semblance of time; she only knows at some point she's ready to find a shattering climax once again when a knocking at the big metallic door brings it all to a depressingly sudden halt.

Knocking.

Not thrashing, clawing, or pounding.

A very controlled, rhythmic, human request for entrance.

"Is somebody in there?" a voice calls from the other side.

It's Little Dove.

"You gotta be fucking kidding me," Dorsky pants into the crook of her neck.

Lena just shakes her head.

"Seriously!" Little Dove persists. "Friend or fucked-up snake thing? Answer me!"

"We're okay!" Lena calls out, hoarsely. "It's Lena. And . . ."

"Dorsky," he says sadly.

Silence from outside.

Then: "Oh."

"Yeah," they say in perfect unison.

"And you guys . . . are yourselves? Have you been

yourselves . . . like, the whole time?"

Again, in unison: "Yeah."

"Okay . . . well . . . you can come out now. If you want. My pop knows how to change everybody back."

That actually causes Lena and Dorsky to separate and stare at the door.

"Seriously?" Lena asks.

"Yeah. He's corralled most of them in one of his weird spirit ancestor force-field deals. Don't ask. I'm going to get Boosha so she can help him mix up some kind of antidote."

No one says anything after that for a time.

"Well," Little Dove announces. "Glad you guys are okay. I'm going to go now. Weirdly, this is the most awkward I've felt all day."

They hear her footfalls carry her away from the door.

A few moments later Dorsky obviously decides to just go for it: "So, do you want to . . . you know . . . keep going? Or—"

"Just get off me."

"Right. Yeah. Good call. Sorry."

They disengage themselves and begin groping for their clothes.

Lena has never been more grateful for an almost complete lack of light and vision.

AIN'T NO CUPCAKE

Unfortunately, any astral memo about White Horse's sudden show of company solidarity doesn't reach Nikki and the rest of the staff trapped in the library in time.

Fortunately, however, that event is preamble to the stuff of legend rather than tragedy.

Later, Pacific and Mr. Mirabal will refer to Nikki's entrance atop the royal wedding cake as "a total hero moment."

Much later than that, Nikki will secretly, although never vocally, agree with them.

The orgy in the reception hall has not lost its proverbial steam, although most of the creatures have lost interest in banging down the staging area doors.

Soon after they stop battering at them, those same doors are forced open by the massive bottom disc of a five-tiered, thirty-foot wedding cake.

Pacific and Mo are concealed inside the cake, pushing it along like a foot-powered stone vehicle from *The Flintstones*.

Prince Marek and Princess Bianca are poised

sentinel-like atop the middle tier, manning opposite edges. They're both armed with the nearly life-sized bride and groom statues that were made to top the cake (perhaps symbolically, perhaps ironically, or perhaps just randomly Bianca cradles the groom while Marek holds aloft the bride).

And standing tall on the cake's summit, stripped to the tank top she wears beneath her smock and that smock now tied around her waist like flour-stained armor, is Nikki. She has bound her elaborately rolled hair in a classic car–emblazoned bandana. In each hand she holds a piping bag bulging with Boosha's "temporary" lust-monster cure. There are half a dozen cooking syringes sheathed through her belt like daggers. The diamond archway topping the cake frames her, and its light dances over the weeping angel tattoo covering most of her right arm and shoulder, making it look like angelic war paint.

She is no less than a confection-armed Valkyrie.

It takes less than thirty seconds for the sight and scent of new flesh to draw the first throng of lustful creatures decimating the reception hall with their violent fornication. A dozen of them sink claws and fangs into the bottom tier of the cake, pulling their monstrous bulk over the first hurdle and scrambling up to the middle tier.

Prince Marek is the first one to make positive contact.

He bats at the first transformed wedding guest to make it within striking distance, not swatting it away from the cake, but bashing it against the cake's frame.

As he does, Nikki leans over the cake top and squeezes the piping bag in her right hand, spraying a cloud of green-brown dust directly over the middle tier.

There's a moment of atom-thin tension during which time slows to a crawl. All three of them remove their focus from the oncoming horde to watch the tattered tuxedo-clad creature now sneezing violently amid a pestilence harvested from high-end appetizers and desserts.

The three of them watch.

And wait.

The hideous, fanged creature being bludgeoned by a four-foot plastic bride suddenly becomes Uncle Ted.

There's relief communicated among all of them without words or a look, but none of them have time to rest on it.

"Baby, look out!" Marek yells at Bianca, and in the next moment they're bludgeoning an entire row of lusting bipedal reptiles.

Nikki aims both piping bags and fills the air around the cake's center with an antidote cloud.

Soon there's a swell of half-dressed human bodies piled against the middle tier, moaning and sweat-covered and dazed to the point of immobility. Marek and Bianca are forced to climb and leap over them to bash the creatures now coming for the transformed. Nikki responds by hopping down three tiers in a row to cover them with more dust, dropping another wave of reverted wedding guests.

The final wave is now crashing through what remains of the tables and buffet to get at the bottom of the wedding cake. Several of them rage right into the now thick cloud of dust and are felled immediately, but more manage to break through it without absorbing enough of the compound to revert.

"I'm out!" Nikki yells, casting away the now empty bladders of the piping bags.

"What now?" Bianca shouts up the tiers as she bashes one of the remaining creatures across the back of its knees, toppling it.

In answer Nikki draws one of the syringes thrust in her belt and stabs it into the head of what turns out to be Bianca's cousin Fabio.

Advancing farther down the cake, Nikki pulls two more syringes and drives them into the nearest frothing creatures, pressing the plunger with her thumbs and reverting them both into a pair of Bianca's in-laws.

A fourth syringe is drawn and hurled seven feet across the bottom cake tier, where it sticks a monster in a bridesmaid's gown, and Marek depresses the plunger by swinging his bride statue into it.

It's an act so amazing Marek and Nikki both stop to acknowledge it by staring at each other, their eyes simultaneously asking, "Did that just fucking happen?"

There are only a few scant stragglers lingering in the background now. Nikki rallies Marek and Bianca, clambering over the writhing, sore bodies returned to human form.

"Take them down!" Nikki commands, syringes at the ready.

The goblin prince and princess systematically batter each remaining creature to the floor, where Nikki impales them.

Ironically, the final guest to be transformed crashed the wedding to hound for autographs.

Nikki holds her final syringe at the ready, suddenly aware there's no one left to inject. Her panicked, adrenaline-pumped brain refuses to accept this at first, but turning and casting her gaze around multiple times confirms it.

"Is it over?" Bianca asks, panting, still clutching her now blood-smeared groom cake-topper.

"I think so," Marek says, a mirror image of her.

They all look out over the battlefield of naked and half-naked bodies, every one of them alive and severely worse for the wear. Some of the first to revert have now collected their facilities and are trilling for help.

It's an unsettling sight.

Then, somewhere beneath the din, a dull, repeating thud.

Someone knocking against the interior of the cake.

"Yo!" Pacific yells, muffled, from within. "I know we got ourselves in here, but I can't remember how!"

Prince Marek, hunched over his bride topper like a crutch, actually smiles. "Those two should have their own sitcom."

Nikki nods, becoming aware for the very first time that from the tops of the library stacks that have been pushed into the back of the space, the goblin guests are cheering wildly for them.

Not one of them has the capacity to laugh at that moment.

Except for Pacific and Mo, who can be heard giggling inside the cake, no doubt over something completely unrelated.

QUITTING TIME

"You have officially and irrevocably done lost your motherfucking mind," Cindy insists.

She's standing in front of Ritter, who has stripped to his bare ass and on whose body Hara is busily and expertly painting arcane runes.

"We've run out of options," he says.

"Not trying to pass through a goddamn magical brick wall is an option. Waiting is an option. Those are two just off the top of my head."

"Your angry, overtly masculine second-in-command has a point, Ritter," Ryland chimes in from his lawn chair.

"Eat me, you lush!" Cindy snaps at him.

"Have you actually pulled this one off before, Ritt?" Bronko asks.

"I've seen it done."

Cindy remains skeptical. "How many times?"

"Once."

"Jesus."

She stomps away from him.

"If you die does it mean we work for Cindy?" Moon

asks. "Because if so, I quit."

"You all work for me," Bronko says. "So shut up, Moon."

He steps close to Ritter, speaking for his ear alone. "Not that I don't appreciate the effort here, but this seems a mite . . . reckless? Even for you. I mean, I've never known you not to hang your ass on a fence post, but you usually do it with more planning."

Hara, painting the last few runes on Ritter's calves, grunts his agreement.

"I'm out of plans," is all Ritter says.

Bronko leans back and stares at Ritter's stoic expression.

"All right, then."

He steps back.

Hara stands, dropping the horsehair brush in the paint can he's been using.

He nods down at Ritter.

His eyes are grave.

"No worries, big man."

Hara remains dubious, but he stands aside.

They all gather behind Ritter, standing shoulder to shoulder, watching his bare, scrawled back intently.

Except for Ryland, of course. He continues to recline on his lawn chair.

He does, however, pour himself a seventh glass of

wine.

Ritter inhales deeply several times, clenching and un-clenching his fists.

He begins chanting inaudibly under his breath.

He stares lethally at the brick barricade where the service entrance should be and on some plane of existence still is.

He runs at the door.

Ritter stops four feet short of collision when the patch of enchanted brick abruptly disappears and in its place a door opens.

Lena is the first one to emerge, laughing at something that was said a moment before.

Dorsky is behind her.

They both stop short, taking in the sight of Ritter naked, painted from head to toe, and panting heavily.

"Whoa," is all Lena manages.

Dorsky is slightly more articulate. "Holy shit, man."

Darren, James, and the other line cooks, along with White Horse and Little Dove, begin filing out behind them.

"Are y'all okay?" Bronko calls to them from across the pavement.

"Yeah, Chef," Dorsky says. "Everyone's whole. The medicine man and Dances in Halter Top there magicked them back to normal."

"Fuck you, Dorsky," Little Dove says.

Lena backhands him in the chest for good measure.

"Sorry," he says, but he's grinning down at Lena.

And she's grinning back.

Ritter watches them, and the sudden connection between them would be apparent to even the least keen observer of the human condition.

He's suddenly very aware he's naked.

"Okay, then," Bronko says. "Lill, I need you and your grandfather to come with me to my trunk. Jett is still in need of your ministrations."

"This is all overtime, you know," White Horse says.

"Pop! Just . . . come on."

The cooks all step aside so White Horse and Little Dove can pass by.

As they do, Lena walks up to Ritter.

"Um . . . is everything okay out here?"

Ritter rests his hands on his hips and nods casually. "Yeah. We figured you'd handle the situation. This was just . . . you know, a backup plan. Just in case."

"You look like someone rolled Silly Putty over the Necronomicon," Dorsky says.

Ritter gives him the finger without looking at him.

His expression remains unchanged.

Lena just nods. "Well. Thanks. Just the same."

"I guess I still owe you one."

"Yeah, I guess so," Lena says. Then, with the briefest of glances downward, "A big one."

That wipes the grin off of Dorsky's face.

IT'S ALL ABOUT THE
AFTERMATH PARTY

"Dear friends and new kin, I give you Prince Marek and Princess Bianca!" the goblin king announces.

The crowd gathered in the wreckage of the reception area, goblin and human alike, cheers raucously.

On stage, Marek and Bianca wave their battered, chipped, and green-blood-smeared cake toppers like ceremonial halberds.

Nikki can't believe how the evening is ending.

She was certain they'd be furious, particularly the king and queen. She was certain the goblin attendees would demand answers, would demand all of the Sin du Jour employees' heads for the near-death-or-at-least-near-reptile-humping experience they were all made to face tonight.

Instead the star of the latest blockbuster superhero movie turns to her, spectacularly drunk and with half his tuxedo stripped away, and joyously yells in her ear, "This is the craziest fuckin' party I've been to since Nicholson spiked everyone's Cristal with vintage biker acid last year!"

He's hardly alone.

None of them seem to mind.

If anything, they're impressed with the heights of mayhem and depravity the wedding attained.

They may be the hierarchy of the goblin world, Nikki realizes, but they're still mostly Hollywood people.

And Hollywood people are severely fucked up.

She has to laugh.

The humans were another matter when most of them took back possession of their sense. They were all sore, and most of them were appalled and angry. Fortunately Jett showed up, looking like hell but clad in a crisp new Chanel suit and ever the determined professional. She had new party attire for the bride and groom, and a mixture from Boosha that not only salved the sex-worn bits of the offended, but drastically improved their moods.

Most of the ones who were complaining the loudest are now swaying arm in arm with the goblin celebrities as they all capitulate before the royal family.

The goblin king motions deftly and the uniformed cast of the CW's newest hit show, *What's a Ghoul to Do,* wheels out a gleaming antique grand piano.

The king sits gracefully at the ivory and ebony keys, speaking into a microphone attached to the unspeakably gorgeous instrument.

"Bianca, my dear," he begins in the sage voice generations of artistic music lovers have worshipped. "Tonight you met adversity and threat with absolute poise and steel. Tonight you truly were the goblin princess. You stood beside your prince and fought for your people. And my son, my prince, my heir, tonight you showed, not that you may rule, but that you may lead. You will both one day be a king and queen whom people may not only revere, but in whom they can take pride."

There isn't a thinking creature alive that could listen to those words in that voice spoken by that man and disagree.

No one in the library does.

The king moves seamlessly into the opening strains of one of his most iconic love songs.

Nikki actually forgets that she just battled a legion of horny snake monsters from atop a two-story wedding cake.

After the song is over, everyone applauds, standing, and the newly married couple make their way offstage and find her in the crowd.

"I know this sounds strange, considering, but thank you so much for everything," Marek says to her.

"The queen hugged me," Bianca whispers in Nikki's ear. "She actually hugged me and called me her daughter!

Can you even? Can you?"

Nikki doesn't know what to say to any of that, so she just smiles and nods and hugs the princess tightly.

"Congratulations," she says to them both.

The newlyweds take to the dance floor with the rest of the assemblage.

"Hey, Nik."

It's Pacific.

"What's up?"

"All the new servers quit. I think one of them did some mouth stuff with a snake dude while the others watched and none of them can deal with it now."

"Wow. Okay. Well, it's not like that doesn't happen all the time, Pac. At least none of them died."

"You're a bright-side kind of chick, and I dig that about you," Pacific says amiably.

"Thank you."

Nikki continues watching Marek and Bianca dance. She takes in the merriment of the drunk goblins and the doped-up humans.

She remembers what she told Lena about working for Sin du Jour.

"Wonders," Nikki whispers to herself.

The party goes until dawn.

A century later they'll still be telling the story of Marek and Bianca's wedding.

It will be considered the epitome of goblin celebration.

EPILOGUE: GENTLE REMINDERS

"Seriously, it's all good, boss man," Jett's voice assures him over Bronko's phone. "I still can't believe it myself, but this will probably be the event they put on my tombstone. And not to condemn me, either."

"That's something, then. Thanks, Jett. No one soldiers like you soldier, kid."

Bronko ends the call and slips the phone into his pocket, continuing up the halls of Sin du Jour.

He just wants fifteen minutes and a stiff drink before he returns to helping his crew put the place back together again.

When Bronko opens the door to his office Allensworth is sitting behind Bronko's desk, spinning in his chair like a little kid attending take-your-child-to-work day.

It's a far more whimsical sight than Bronko would ever associate with the straight-up-and-down government spook.

He's not quite sure what to make of it.

Allensworth stops spinning.

He smiles gently up at Bronko.

"Good evening, Byron."

Allensworth has never once referred to him as "Bronko," and if he were to start it would probably make the executive chef hate his lifelong nickname.

"The chairs in your office don't spin?" Bronko asks.

Allensworth laughs. "They don't, in fact. They don't. Forgive me. I've been waiting a goodly while. I became bored."

Bronko stands across the desk and folds his arms.

"That sounds like the life to me."

Allensworth nods. "I suppose it does after the events of the day. My, what an absolute classically Mongolian clusterfuck that wedding was."

"These things happen."

"They've been happening quite a bit lately, haven't they?"

"I don't take your meaning."

"Oh, Byron," Allensworth chastises him, rising from the chair and moving slowly around the desk. "You don't honestly think we're unaware of your ruse with the seraphim, do you?"

It's been a long time since Bronko's poker face has been tested to this degree.

He'll never know how well it held up.

Allensworth faces him, only inches away.

His smile is unwavering.

"Your sentimentality is understandable, even admirable, but it was horribly misplaced. Still and all, there was no real harm done. But this latest incident . . . beyond the embarrassment it has caused my department, me personally, and Sin du Jour, it posed a very serious threat to our security. All of our security."

"We contained it."

"It was contained. I wouldn't necessarily say 'we' contained it."

"You locked my people in here and left them to die. I'm of a mind to be awful upset about that. How about we both let things go and move forward?"

Allensworth shakes his head. "I answer to more than myself, Byron. Vastly more. Now, I'm uncertain what if anything has changed around here, or if perhaps you've changed—"

"I'm doing the job I was hired to do."

"And you always do. Excellently. I simply want to ensure that that continues, and that the events of our recent Oexial parlay and royal wedding do not become a trend."

"Consider yourself assured, then."

"I appreciate that, Byron. I do. However, I am a staunch believer in motivation. Proper motivation."

Bronko's jaw locks immediately and his heart begins racing.

"I think you'd be served by a gentle reminder, Byron. Of your contract. Of your obligations. Of the penalties for failing either."

Bronko is already shaking his head before Allensworth has finished speaking.

"Look, we don't need to do this—"

He never sees Allensworth move, nor does Bronko feel the blade until it has pierced the large portal vein in his abdomen. Even then it feels like nothing more than a severe cramp. The pain causes him to double over slightly and look down at Allensworth's hand wrapped around the nondescript hilt of a dagger, most of which has disappeared inside Bronko's stomach.

When he looks up the expression on Allensworth's face hasn't changed. His smile is easy and friendly, his eyes utterly unperturbed.

It's as if his face is completely disconnected from the actions of the rest of his body.

Allensworth expertly slips the blade free of Bronko's body cavity.

The blood flow is torrential.

The strength leaves Bronko's legs. Everything below his waist feels cold, a cold that quickly spreads throughout the rest of him.

As he slumps to his office floor, Allensworth turns to the desk and takes up a random piece of paper, sandwiching the thin, double-edged blade in his hand between it and wiping it clean.

Allensworth delicately crumples the stained piece of paper and drops it into the nearest wastebasket.

The dagger disappears back under his pressed jogging jacket.

Bronko is lying on his side now. His instinct is to apply pressure to the bleeding with his hands, but both of his arms refuse to obey his commands.

It's almost impossible for him to keep his eyes open.

He is, however, able to watch Allensworth's sneaker-clad feet as he quietly exits the office, humming a tune Bronko can't really hear.

He closes the door behind him.

The world seems to be made of blood now.

It's everywhere, on Bronko and surrounding him, filling his vision.

He doesn't know it, but he has fifteen seconds to live.

Fifteen seconds is an eternity to those who trade in magic.

It's plenty of time for any one of the dozens of loyal employees of Sin du Jour to stumble into Bronko's office and find him slouching to death's door.

It's more than enough time for them to summon the magic to save him, or summon a coworker who can do the same.

Unfortunately none of these things happen.

No one comes.

Fifteen seconds pass in a few ragged, terrified breaths.

Bronko dies.

SMALL WARS

This story first appeared on *Tor.com* in January 2016

NOW—CARDIFF AIRPORT, WALES

"And what do you do in America?" the customs agent asks Ritter, staring at the nondescript man's passport.

"I'm a steward. I work for a catering company in New York City."

"Is that like a host, then?"

"No."

The customs agent looks up from the official document and stares at him. There's nothing aggressive or short in Ritter's tone, but his passivity, something wholly and comfortably removed, is somehow always more disconcerting for people.

"I'm head of stocking and receiving. You could say I keep the cupboards full," Ritter explains just as passively.

Recognition that's really little more than a scant point of reference widens the custom agent's eyes.

"Ah, I see. And are you here on vacation, then?"

"No. Business."

"Right. Well, if you're planning on returning with any of our local fruit and veg or the like you know you'll have to declare it."

"I'm not here for either. No worries."

"All right, then." Ritter's passport is returned. "Welcome to Wales, Mister Thane."

"Thank you."

Ritter stashes his passport and picks up his aging rucksack.

———————

Within two hours of arriving in Wales, Cindy O'Brien is convinced the Welsh language has been conceived solely as a practical joke played on tourists.

"They're making that shit up as they go along," she insists. "There's nothing even vaguely consistent about a single motherfucking word I've heard said or written on a sign so far. And that includes every word spoken in English."

There are five of them in the rented Ford Transit cargo van: Ritter and the three other members of Sin du Jour Catering & Events' stocking and receiving department, and the freelance alchemist who has joined them for this particular assignment.

Ritter is behind the wheel. Moon, diminutive and poorly groomed and perpetually clad in a dirty T-shirt representing some bit of cultural arcana (today it's a Turkish soccer team) is riding shotgun. This was agreed upon by the others less because he called it and more to convince him to *stop* calling it every time they crossed a new time zone.

Cindy sits behind him, earbuds firmly in place as she attempts to finish the audiobook of Toni Morrison reading her essays that she was unable to finish on the plane due to a constant stream of disruptions around her.

Ryland Phelan, the rumpled-from-head-to-toe Irishman seated next to her both on the plane and in the van now, caused most of those disruptions.

Utterly filling the final row of seats behind them is Hara, the mountainous fourth member of Ritter's team and the eternal stoic.

Ryland drunkenly cranes his neck to focus on Cindy in the loosest possible way. "That presupposes the Welsh are in possession of something recognizable to the civilized world as a sense of humor. I can't imagine a more dangerous assumption."

"Don't even get me started with you again, Jesus of Nazawrecked," she warns him.

"What?" He seems genuinely confused. "What have I done?"

Cindy yanks her earbuds out. "Are you kidding me? Are you so wasted you don't remember being drawn down on by a damn air marshal midflight?"

Ryland's red eyes widen. "Was that who that irate gentleman was? Well, that makes much more sense, then."

After having his beverage service cut off less than two hours after takeoff, Ryland began requesting cups of water and changing them into white wine.

The only reason they weren't all detained upon arrival was because, when confronted, the air marshal couldn't find any hidden supply of alcohol or a corresponding empty vessel.

"Did we have to bring him?" Cindy asks Ritter. "He couldn't have just given you instructions and some of his funky stones?"

"Growing gold from bare rock is a little advanced for me, Cin," Ritter informs her.

Ryland is genuinely offended. "I would expect more than a cheap rebuke such as that from a fellow countryman . . . person . . . thing. You know."

"I am none of that."

"You may not possess my rustic brogue, but 'O'Brien' speaks of Irish ancestry."

"Black Irish," Moon adds with his typical lack of taste, sensitivity, or actual knowledge.

Cindy thrusts the flat of her palm into the back of his head hard enough that he has to shake off the blow afterward.

"That's not even what 'black Irish' means, you little shit."

"She hit me again," Moon complains to Ritter.

"You deserved it again."

"Children," Cindy curses them under her breath, replacing her earbuds. "All of you. Fucking children."

2011—LAS VEGAS, NEVADA

The ballroom of The Pirate's Doubloon Hotel and Casino, miles from the Strip.

Home to countless cold-roast-beef-and-string-bean Shriners convention dinners, arts and crafts expos, and wedding receptions bereft of a single tuxedo.

A vinyl banner that was printed at FedEx Kinko's proclaims the event to be *"Hot Zones* 3rd Annual International Combat Knife-Fighting Tournament" in a discontinued Windows font. About two hundred people are in attendance for the popular so-called "mercenary" magazine's keystone yearly event. The walls are lined with merchandising tables crewed by knife dealers, survivalists handing out pamphlets ranging from useful to paranoid to batshit, and several companies hocking paintball warrior weekends and related "experiences."

Ritter enters the scene just in time for the finals of the tournament that has lasted for two days and drawn competitors from all over the world (and in true "all over the world" fashion, 90 percent of those competitors are

Americans, who've been joined by a handful of Scandinavians on holiday, a surly German war fetishist, and a Filipino ex-soldier whose entire village took up a collection to send him to the tournament).

The final two competitors stand shirtless in the ring. Cindy wears a basic black sports bra, while her male opponent is allowed to freely flaunt his nonfunctioning nipples. They both have numbers scrawled on their stomachs in thick red marker, and they're armed with knives fashioned from hard nylon that are typically used in training and demonstrations.

They wear no protective gear.

This isn't a safety-oriented crowd.

Their ring is composed of four elongated plastic folding tables arranged in a haphazard square, allowing them just enough room to maneuver. Two referees in *Hot Zones* T-shirts observe the match from different angles.

Cindy's opponent is a determined-looking Jicarilla Apache who has traveled to the tournament with a small battalion of supporters from the reservation, all of them wearing T-shirts that declare them "Team Perea."

When one of the refs gives them the command, the two finalists begin slashing at each other, dipping forward and leaping back with frantic speed. There's some technique to be seen among the spastic feints and strikes, but actual combat is a messy, disjointed affair. Speed and determination often win out over casual martial-arts training.

Cindy is a pit bull, her knife hand obsessively going for her opponent's throat. Each time the plastic blade connects with flesh the referees separate the two of them and award her a point.

They fight to five points.

Cindy harmlessly slashes Perea's throat five times without positive contact from his blade even once.

When the final point is awarded no one in the crowd seems particularly happy she's won.

Unsurprising, considering she's one of maybe five women in a ballroom of two hundred men.

The top prize is fifteen thousand dollars. Within four hours of accepting her title and check Cindy has gambled half of the money away in the casino. Ritter observes her from a safe distance the whole time. She pounds rum and cokes with alarming rapidity and rarely speaks to anyone around her.

When she anoints herself too buzzed to make rational card-playing decisions, Cindy retreats to a video poker machine far away from the nearest other patron.

That's where Ritter approaches her, taking a seat in front of the machine one removed from her own.

"You want something?" she asks him after a few awkward minutes.

Ritter nods. "I do. I want to hire you."

"What I look like to you, dude?"

"A soldier."

That statement briefly takes Cindy aback, and then she looks down at the exposed ink on her arms. An Explosive Ordinance Disposal "crab" badge is tattooed on her right forearm while a navy anchor whose shaft is a lit stick of dynamite opposes it on her left.

"All right," she says, more composed. "So what?"

"So I'm going to talk for sixty seconds, and if you want to hear more I'll be in the McDonald's in back of this shit-hole waiting with two cups of coffee. Fair enough?"

Cindy shrugs. "Whatever."

"You're what, six months out? You're drifting. You're drinking too much. You're gambling too much. You can't remember the name of anyone you've fucked since your discharge because you never really asked their name in the first place."

Cindy starts at that, angrily, but when she searches his expression for some bullshit gender-based judgment she finds none.

She realizes he sounds like he's speaking from experience.

She realizes he's one soldier speaking to another.

"You're still a soldier," he continues. "That's all you

want to be. You're not built for civilian life, but that's where you are. You need a mission. But with your service record the only mission anyone is going to give you would be wiring the car of a drug lord or sweeping the caravan of some profiteering corporate fuck overseas. And you don't want that. Because despite why they booted you, you have a conscience."

"Who the fuck are you?" she asks him, on the verge of tears.

"I can offer you a mission you can be proud of. One that's about serving people instead of blowing them to hell and gone. It's straight work. It's well-paid work. And I'll never ask you to do anything that will make you hate yourself."

Ritter stands up. "That was a little more than sixty seconds, but I thought that pitched better. Like I said, I'll be in the McDonald's over there."

Ritter exits the casino. He crosses the hotel lobby to the small food court that operates twenty-four hours. He orders two large coffees from the McDonald's kiosk and occupies a table in the common area.

He waits.

Cindy joins him before the coffee has cooled.

NOW

They drive northwest, to Bontddu, near Barmouth, in Gwynedd.

None of them except Hara have any idea how to pronounce the names, and he doesn't feel the need to comment.

They pass the more famous Clogau mine, which remains active to this day. A few short decades ago there was still as much as five hundred thousand ounces of gold waiting to be unearthed in its bowels, but since the late nineties it's been mined completely dry.

They drive off the beaten path to a far less known, smaller mine that has been abandoned for years since its veins ran dry. It's removed and set against a Tolkien-esque wilderness.

Ritter halts the van and they all get out, Ryland reluctantly and uncoordinatedly. They pull coveralls on over their clothes, fitting the straps of air filtration masks around their necks and attaching devices to their forearms that monitor air-toxicity levels.

The entrance to the abandoned mine isn't simply boarded up, it has been blasted shut. Behind the dusty, rotted wood planks is a wall of tightly packed-in boulders of varying shape and size.

Hara helps Cindy unload a portable drill press attached to an eight-foot-high jack from the back of the Transit. The drill's bit is diamond a half-inch thick. As they wheel it up to the entrance Ritter and Moon use crowbars to pry away the boards zigzagging the collapsed rock face.

"If I can be of any service at this point in the proceedings you'll inform me immediately, yeah?" Ryland calls from where he's reclining against the open back of the van.

"I really dislike him," Cindy casually informs Ritter.

"He dislikes himself more, I promise you."

Cindy cranks the press several feet up the jack and begins drilling a hole through one of the boulders packed in the entranceway. She repositions the press seven more times and drills seven more holes at various points and heights in the obstruction.

Once that's done, she removes and uncaps several airtight containers from one of the main rucksacks in the van. She pulls out thin lines of high-tensile cord, the ends of which are weighted with thin cylinders. Attached to the lines at three-foot intervals are what look like compressed wads of tissue paper drenched in bright pink liquid.

Cindy carefully and meticulously begins feeding each line through a hole she's drilled in the rock.

"Is the van out of your blast path?" Ritter asks her.

She never takes her eyes off her work or halts her hands. "Yeah, we're good. It shouldn't push the debris past a twenty-foot diameter. It should mostly just collapse."

"I'm hearing *should* a lot," Moon comments from the sidelines.

No one says anything, but Hara stares down at him with a rare showing of emotion, that emotion being highly annoyed.

Moon shuts up.

"All right, we're ready to go hot," Cindy announces. "Everybody behind the van."

They all obey, joining Ryland who already has two cigarette butts crushed into the ground at his feet.

Cindy reaches inside her coveralls and removes an iPhone.

"Moon, if you ask me if I have an app for this I'll perforate your chest cavity with my middle and forefinger," she warns him in a neutral tone.

"You're still pissed about the black-Irish thing, aren't you?"

"Yes, I am," Cindy says, and taps the iPhone's screen.

The blast itself isn't loud, but the sound of the rocks breaking apart is particularly grating on their ears. Debris no bigger than pebbles sprawls down the hill, none of it touching the van.

What's left is a pile of rubble that rises to about half the height of the entranceway.

The darkness beyond is now visible.

"Artful as always, Cin," Ritter tells her.

For the first time since arriving in Wales, she smiles.

Hara is able to clear away most of the rubble with a shovel before the rest of them have even retrieved theirs. Instead, Ritter passes out the rest of the gear and large digital torches to each of them.

"It smells like a Welshman's arse," Ryland complains.

"I look forward to that chapter in your memoirs," Cindy says.

"Let's go, Ryland," Ritter bids him. "You're on."

Removing the current lit cigarette from his mouth and flicking it away with a sigh, Ryland enters the mine ahead of them.

"Why gold?" he demands as they trek through the main shaft. "Why must they eat gold?"

"Matters of goblin digestion don't concern me," Ritter says. "This is the job."

"Why Welsh gold, then?"

"Because it's the rarest in the world and it's a royal goblin wedding. They want the best."

"Overcompensating gombeens," Ryland mutters.

He reaches inside his coveralls and removes a large gemstone.

Even in the almost total darkness it gleams bloodred.

Ryland begins holding it up against the walls of the shaft as they tread along.

"So you're really going to grow new gold here?" Moon asks him.

"Theoretically."

"Even though there's none left in this pit?"

"Traces enough remain."

"And it'll be real? The gold?"

"As real as the odor now assaulting us."

"I don't get it. If you can literally fucking grow gold, why the hell are you working at Sin du Jour?"

"Alchemic karma," Ryland says as if that's all the explanation required.

"What the hell is that?"

"If I attempted to profit personally the gold would turn to shite. Literally."

"That sounds made-up."

"If it wasn't a very real thing do you imagine I'd currently be dwelling in a disused recreational vehicle behind a catering firm in Long Island City?"

Moon thinks about that.

"Yeah. Fair enough."

Someone snickers in the dark.

It might even be Hara.

The gem in Ryland's hand begins pulsing.

"What the devil—"

He pauses.

"What's up?" Ritter asks. "You find a vein?"

"No, that's not what this means."

"Then what does it mean?" Cindy asks with alarm.

Ryland turns to the anterior wall, squinting into the darkness.

There isn't a single break in the rock, yet somehow a golf ball–sized sphere of rusted metal emerges from the wall of the chamber, flies across the space, and cracks him in the left temple.

He falls.

Hard.

Dozens upon dozens of spheres begin firing through the wall, brutally pelting them. Ritter, Moon, and Cindy break for the side walls, trying to clear the strike path.

In the next moment Hara is there over Ryland, his back to the sphere-spewing rock, scooping up the drunken alchemist as easily as a father picking up his toddler.

"Go!" Ritter orders him. "Get him out!"

Hara hesitates for less time than can be practically measured, then charges back down the entrance shaft.

"What the fuck—" Moon yells before catching a sphere in the face and dropping to a fetal ball at Ritter's feet.

Ritter looks down, shining his light on a half-dozen of the assaulting objects as they roll to a halt and unfurl themselves.

They're not spheres.

They're tiny bipedal beings.

Each one is the height of an index finger, bearded and with flesh that looks as hard as the rock from which they emerged. Their entire bodies and all their appendages are adorned with curved pieces of armor obviously designed to become near-solid spheres when tucked together.

As he looks on, the armored creatures begin dog-piling one another, more spheres rolling to join what at first looks like a chaotic mass of metal but soon begins to take a definite shape. The sound of tumblers falling in a lock echoes throughout the chamber as the small armored figures interlock with one another, their mass building in height and defining in shape until it begins to resemble a full-sized human form.

Ritter's seen enough. He turns to grab Cindy, but sudden streaks of color crackling with repellent energy knock him back, separating them.

It looks like a wall of rainbow-colored caution tape has been unfurled in front of him.

Ritter turns from it to find himself face-to-face with a gargantuan automaton fashioned from hundreds of armored bodies; they've even arranged themselves to give it a vague double-wide face with hollow eyes and curving lips.

"All right, that's a new one on me," Ritter says, and it sounds like a disturbingly casual admission under the circumstances.

The construct doesn't banter with him.

In the next moment Ritter's casual demeanor has turned dire as he ducks and rolls from the path of a sweeping metallic limb intent on decapitating him. Ritter bounces to his feet, now behind the automaton, curling his right arm and driving the thick ulna bone of his forearm into the thing's many-eyed "back."

It's a blow that would painfully readjust the spine of a human opponent.

This opponent, however, has no spine and a backside made of modular refined ore from the bowels of the Earth.

As such, the impact bruises Ritter's forearm down to the bone, which also splinters and sends chemical signals of agony to his brain.

Ritter steps back, half a dozen curse words blending into one unintelligible oath that only ends when he has to duck to avoid the automaton's next swing as it turns around.

The construct advances on him, Ritter backpedaling and scantly avoiding several more blows. He feints and ducks the metal limbs, the facilities of his mind generally tasked with such things collectively shrugging at him as he requests a plan of action.

"Oh, fuck it!" he yells out loud.

Ritter ducks under the next swing and dips briefly against the construct's body, reaching out with both hands and gripping one of the interconnected armored creatures balled up there. With a berserker's cry and every ounce of strength he can muster, he rips the sphere free of the rest of its fellow and leaps back.

The act causes the briefest moment of confusion among the rest of the things composing the creature's body.

More important, it causes the briefest moment of hesitation.

Ritter jumps back in, still holding the armored ball, and smashes its surface against the "face" of the construct, detaching several other spheres from their host and sending them flying.

He immediately reverses the position of the armored ball in his hand and backhands the other side of the construct's "face," depleting it further. Ritter continues bashing it with a piece of itself until finally he drops down and smashes the best approximation of a knee joint he can locate on one of the thing's "legs."

The construct is forced to one knee.

A grating chatter, like a thousand squeaking voices, rises from its every nonexistent pore.

It's a confused sound.

It's vulnerable sound.

It's stopped lashing out.

Ritter rears back for a coup de grâce, but halts as his entire body abruptly seizes, pain shooting up through his arm. He turns to look at his hand and can't help freezing further to marvel at the sight of a much tinier hand protruding out from the armored sphere.

That tiny hand is holding an even tinier dagger.

That tinier dagger is buried in the meat of Ritter's palm.

As he squints in puzzlement at the sight, the tiny hand twists the tinier dagger.

Ritter curses and drops the sphere altogether. He hears it skitter over the dank, rocky terra and in his anger and pain scans the ground in the dark, hoping to crush the thing underfoot.

An eternity might as well have passed by the time he remembers his main opposition isn't the thing that stabbed him.

It's behind him.

And the confused chatter has ceased.

Ritter already knows he won't have time to turn around, but he tries anyway.

The gargantuan construct raises a four-fingered hand and swings it into the side of Ritter's head, breaking itself apart and sending a dozen bearded warriors flying upon contact.

Their elated hollers are the last thing Ritter hears before the darkness takes him.

2009—ALGERIA

The average Westerner finds little reason to travel to the Saharan interior of North Africa, much less the middle of the desert, life-threatening miles from anything resembling civilization.

Ritter has never been average in any respect.

As such he currently finds himself staring at a horizon made of fire in the hottest season of the year, when there's not a cloud to be seen in the sky and the air is so dry it sucks at every pore like a thousand microscopic vampires.

His guide is an ancient, withered Igbo man draped in a woefully oversized Isiagu who sits in the back of their jeep obsessively playing Angry Birds on his smartphone.

"How much longer, you figure?" Ritter asks him.

"Not long now," the old man's raspy voice replies while its owner never takes his eyes from the tiny screen.

"They will come for the water."

"What water?"

"The water beneath our feet."

"Oh." Ritter looks down at the seemingly unending sand. "And how long is 'not long,' again?"

"Soon."

This followed by an inaudible curse and some kind of digital rebuke from the man's game.

Ritter nods. "Right."

He looks back at the horizon.

Three hours later a trio of figures on horseback appears out of the illusory blaze. They descend and gallop toward the spot where Ritter and his guide have parked their vehicle.

As they close the gap Ritter can see the blue veils covering their faces, stark even in the waning sun. Two of them are Berber while the third is the largest human being Ritter has ever observed. He sits astride a horse twice the size of the others' mounts, and it still looks burdened by the man's weight.

"I tell you," Ritter's guide says, followed by a cluck of victory as he reaches a new level in his ceaseless game. "Soon."

"You're the man, Diji," Ritter assures him.

The riders halt several yards from their position, and the giant urges his mount forward, away from the other two. When he's within a few feet of Ritter he climbs from his saddle, momentarily blotting out the sun.

"The whole desert-rider mystique works for you, man," Ritter tells him. "How're the Touaregs treating you?"

Hara doesn't answer, but Ritter doesn't expect him to.

Instead he removes his veil. His wide features aren't painted with the brush of Africa, any part of it. He's clearly a hybrid, but there's more of Mongolia in his face than anything.

Hara waits.

"I need you," Ritter says. "I don't know for how long."

Hara nods.

Without a word he leads his horse by the reins back to his Berber companions and turns them over to one of them.

For the first time, Diji looks up from Angry Birds.

"Does the big one owe you a life or something?"

"Something," is all Ritter says.

NOW

He comes to with a hundred tiny pains in his wrists, a dry mouth, a throbbing cranium, and a pore-seeping feeling in every inch of his skin.

"You know," Moon says miserably beside him, "this job is the big sweaty tits right up until it absolutely fucking sucks."

Ritter blinks away dampness and waits calmly for his eyes to adjust to the relative dark.

They're in a small chamber with no apparent entrances or exits. They're both pressed against an unnaturally smooth wall of rock, and their hands are bound above their heads by what seem like natural formations, as if their wrists have been there for millennia and four thick bands of stone have shaped around them.

Or they're restraints fashioned by tiny magical creatures that can manipulate the Earth.

"Where are Cindy and the others?" Ritter asks him.

"Fucked if I know. I woke up with a headache just like you. And I'm not even gonna try to explain what I saw back in the mine shaft."

Ritter nods.

They wait.

It's not like in the movies, when prisoners awaken and their captors march right in to explain everything.

They wait a long fucking time.

It sucks.

Eventually there's a gentle rumbling and a barrage of the metallic spheres emerges seamlessly from the far wall, landing on the ground and rolling to a halt in perfect unison. Each sphere unfurls and they begin to interlock themselves into the cyborg-automaton form that attacked Ritter and the team back in the mine shaft.

It's somehow even more unsettling, standing there inert, a thousand tiny eyes staring at them while the hollow shapes of two large eyes appear to blink in the thing's "face."

"We are the Gnomi," a voice made up of each individual creature speaking in unison announces.

"Yeah, I kind of figured that," Ritter says. "I've never seen a gnome, but I wouldn't exactly have pegged you for pond sprites."

"Are you in league with the Tuath Dé?" the choral voice of the gnomes asks Ritter.

"No."

"Then what are a human warrior and his squire doing in such a place forsaken by your kind?"

Moon is irate. "Squire? What, like I'm his medieval secretary or some shit? Whoa, hold the fucking phone—"

"Shut up, Moon." And to the creature: "I'm not a warrior. I'm a gatherer."

"You wear the scars of many battles. You hold the death of many enemies in your eyes."

"Gathering has become a rough business up there."

"Then you aren't mercenaries retained by the Tuath

Dé?"

"No."

The gnome construct pauses. The hundreds of them composing its body seem to whisper among themselves before answering in their unified voice.

"Good. You are a great warrior, whatever your protestations to the contrary. You nearly bested the Gnomi in our horde form. No human has ever come so close. You're worthy. Consider yourself conscripted."

Ritter sighs.

Moon looks at him expectantly.

"They want us to fight for them," Ritter explains.

"Just you," the Gnomi correct him. "The little one is of no use. He will be a gift to the rocks."

"What the fuck does that mean?" Moon demands in horror.

"He's my squire," Ritter says quickly, resolutely. "He serves me in battle. He's experienced. Broken in. I don't fight without him."

Silence.

Then: "Very well. Consider yourselves *both* conscripts."

"I don't know what your conflict is down here, but we want no part of it. We just came to forage. We didn't know this was your . . . domain."

"It's too late for such concerns. We've met with our

enemies and agreed upon the hour and place of our final battle. The Tuath Dé have no doubt already conscribed a giant of their own to fight in that upcoming battle. With such an advantage they'll crush us. Unless we have giants to fight for our cause."

"Cindy," Ritter whispers to himself, wanting to smash his own head against the wall behind it.

"What the hell do you need us for?" Moon demands. "You're all magic and shit. You move through solid rock, which appears to be your total bitch."

"The Tuath Dé have their own magic. And try as we might, small magic never seems to win out over giant meat."

That last spoken so bitterly, suggesting eons of learning that lesson over and over.

"There is nothing to discuss," they pronounce with finality. "You will die in battle fighting with the Gnomi or you will die in this room as interlopers. Choose."

"Hey, I'm all for championing a good cause," Moon says immediately. "You should see my Gears of War rankings."

Ritter glances over at him with open disdain.

"Wise choice, humans," the gnome construct says, and in the wake of those words begins disassembling into hundreds of the furry, rock-faced armored creatures.

"Squire?" Moon whispers to Ritter.

"Would you rather be a 'gift' to the rocks?"

"Right. Fine. What the hell is a 'ta-wath' whatever?"

Ritter sighs. "Tuath Dé," Ritter pronounces flawlessly. "It means 'Tribe of the Gods.' They're more popularly known as—"

―――――――

"Leprechauns," Cindy practically spits in anger. "Fucking leprechauns. I've been trussed up with rainbow beams by a bunch of goddamn Lucky Charms four-leaf clover motherfucking leprechauns. I cannot even . . ."

She's berating herself more than speaking to the assemblage of tiny creatures gathered a few yards from her feet. Cindy futilely tugs at the multicolored beams of pure energy binding her wrists behind her back. It doesn't feel as if solid matter is restraining her, yet she can't move it.

Leprechauns are as physically far removed from gnomes as possible, excluding their relative size. Each one is lithe with an angular, almost antlike face. They're naked save for leaves tied as loincloths and shredded into wreathlike hats that strongly resemble bowlers.

Which answers the question of where that bit of imagery came from.

In truth, Cindy is less interested in the assemblage of

magical creatures at her feet and more drawn by the far corners of the cavernous space.

They're filled with gold.

Mounds of it.

Mounds as tall as ancient oak trees.

She can't even begin to calculate the worth of the fortune in direct view.

More than that, it looks almost forgotten, cast aside as if it were all shoved there to get it out of the way. The golden mounds are covered in the dirt and dust of immense age and utter neglect.

But then, what good is gold in the bowels of the Earth?

That's the brief, obvious conclusion at which she arrives.

A fractal ribbon bursts forth from the tiny ranks spread out before her and its lip unfurls to within an inch of her chin.

One of the creatures, feminine to Cindy's perception, practically glides up the beam until she is staring up her nose. She raises a wicked-looking spear.

"We are the Tuath Dé. We were gods when your people were covered in fur and copulating in the muck."

The leprechaun isn't actually speaking, Cindy realizes.

In point of fact she's hearing her words inside her

head, which may in fact be translating their meaning for her for all she knows.

"Well, I seem to recall killing God seven, eight times before you took me down," Cindy answers aloud.

"And you'll pay for each death!"

In reply Cindy works up a wad of spittle and hocks a loogie equivalent to a Buick at the tiny god who has gotten in her face.

It blasts the leprechaun like a fire hose, knocking her halfway down the rainbow-colored beam. It takes several attempts for her to right herself, slathered from head to toe in sticky, viscous spittle.

With a shrill battle cry the leprechaun charges back up the illusory ribbon and slashes Cindy above her right eye, splitting her brow open deep enough to expose bone. Blood quickly begins filling her eye.

Cindy grits her teeth, shutting her eyelid against the sudden, warm flood.

"You great ape," the leprechaun rages. "You're no better than those rock worms, with your stone and steel dwellings. Once my kin built great cities of pure gold that spanned oceans—"

"That's not possible," Cindy interrupts, sounding more annoyed than anything. "Even as small as you are there isn't enough gold in the world—"

"That spanned oceans!" the creature insists. "Your

kind melted them down. We were forced beneath the canopy at their feet, and now they drive us from that to these pitiful mud veins, and even here we must fight the Gnomi for what cramped space is available to us."

"Yeah, you're right," Cindy replies blandly. "What would a black woman know about having her history and culture stolen and raped for hundreds of years?"

The leprechaun either doesn't understand or ignores the statement. "We use what remains to live and to fight. That now includes you. We go to meet the Gnomi in battle."

"So what?"

"They have taken their own giants as prisoners. We saw the big one in battle. He's a fierce fighter. The Gnomi love conscripting dangerous creatures to fight for them. And as you said, you killed a score of our own. You're also a great warrior. We must battle giants with giants. You will fight for us."

"The fuck I will."

The leprechaun presses the tip of her spear into the pulsing center of flesh covering Cindy's carotid artery. It must sound like the beating of a war drum to her.

"You will fight, or you will die. In bondage. If you be a warrior, you'll want to die on your feet with your axe in your hand. So you will fight."

"Those boys are my comrades and my friends. I won't

fight them."

"Then they'll kill you. On your feet. With your axe in your hand. But in the end your kind always fights. You kill everything, until there's nothing left."

The leprechaun raises her spear.

Cindy flinches.

This time, however, a tiny crimson ribbon, like a thin stream of blood underwater, flits from the tip and touches Cindy's wound, closing it.

"The touch of a god," the leprechaun says wryly. "If only your kind appreciated it instead of damning it."

———————

The gnome's name is Auch and he looks ancient even for a creature made of grizzled beard and stony flesh.

"I was a prisoner of your kind for a time," he explains as he balances on Ritter's shoulder.

It's not the high-pitched helium voice of a microscopic character in a fantasy film. It sounds more like an aged whisper.

"I learned to speak your modern tongue. Brought it back to the Gnomi. Comes in handy when some wiseass plastic-helmet-wearing worker bungles into these shafts."

The old gnome grinds the granite meat of his own palm into a fine powder and sprinkles it on Ritter's wounds.

The Gnomi want them both in optimal condition for the battle.

"Why live so close to the surface with the kind of power you have?" Ritter asks. "Everything I've heard about elementals has them dwelling much deeper."

Auch sighs. "Once we kept the whole world spinnin'," he says, the single gnomish voice barely a whisper to them both. "'Twas our task. We formed and re-formed and moved the great rocks to keep the surface from tearing itself asunder. We moved the great wheel of its core to keep it from being spun off into oblivion."

"What happened?" Ritter asks.

"The world changed. The need for elementals lessened. The core became molten. The heat gave rise to creatures like the ones who fathered your kind. We were forced farther and farther from the fire."

Auch works his way around to Ritter's other shoulder, concentrating on his wounds. "Yessir. The Earth you've made is not a place for gnome nor sylph nor salamander anymore. The undine'll be next. When you've spoiled the land you'll delve to new depths of the sea. You don't know no better."

Ritter has nothing to offer that assessment, or its truth.

"Why fight the Tuath Dé? Why not band together to

make the most of what's left?"

"They still think they're gods. We still think we're the wardens of the Earth. Nowhere shall the two meet, I reckon. So we'll keep killing each other over who's the right to these miserable mined-out hollows till we make slaves of the few of them're left or they do the same to us. And there'll come a time when those that've survived the battle to come fade into the rock and that'll be the end of us both."

"Wow," Moon says weightily (for him, anyway). "That's some fucked-up shit, little dude."

"I'm sorry for everything that's happened to your people," Ritter says. "I really am."

Auch snickers. "Aye. Your folk always are. Shame they never feel that way before they do a thing."

"Is it always like this when the lot of you go out?" Ryland asks.

He's sitting on the ground, one hand cradling a half-smoked cigarette while the other holds a clotting, blood-soaked compress against his skull.

Hara doesn't answer.

He's busy smashing a heavy pickax against the cave-in that's preventing them from searching for the others.

"I'll abstain from now on, if it's all the same to you," Ryland adds.

Hara just grunts.

Whether it's a reply or a sign of exertion from bringing the ax against the rock futilely and for the three hundredth time is unclear.

———

Neither Ritter nor Moon can guess how deep beneath the surface they are now, but they both feel as far removed from the world above, their world, as they ever have in their lives.

The Gnomi and the Tuath Dé have chosen a vast, stalagmite-filled cavern as their epic battlefield. The armies are mustered on opposite sides of it. They're too small to take a proper counting, but there can't be more than five hundred in either force.

Ritter wonders fleetingly if those numbers represent their entire respective species.

If the lives of his team weren't in immediate peril he might be filled with sorrow and sympathy for both collectives.

"Is there a plan here, boss?" Moon asks nervously.

"For you? Stay in the background and try not to get killed."

"Check. What are you going to do?"

"Get to Cindy. Try to hack our way out of here. Keep an eye on us."

Ritter stares at Cindy across the subterranean cavern. She looks very much the way she did when he first put eyes on her, stripped to the waist and prepared for combat, only this time, rather than a plastic knife, she's armed with the razor-edged tomahawk he once gifted her.

He can't read her expression.

He doubts she can read his, either.

2012—TIJUANA, MEXICO

"*Hígado del chupacabra!*" the fat master of ceremonies announces, holding a slick, fetid organ high before plopping it down on the tabletop between Moon and his opponent.

The crowd packing the tiny bar cheers raucously as bet takers move through their ranks exchanging hand-scrawled tickets for cash.

Moon is too busy sucking the pickled scorpion from a bottle of mescal to fully take in his next challenge.

His opponent, however, a fierce looking curandera who must be pushing eighty years of age, is focused solely and intently on the piece of offal between them. She grips a knife and fork in her withered fists and steels herself.

Somewhere in the back of the bar Ritter wedges himself between drunken tourists and sober locals. He spots an American in a floral resort shirt flirting with one of the bartenders and wades to him.

"Migs!" Ritter yells through the cacophony.

The man dressed for a Hawaiian vacation turns at the sound of his name and grins wide when he spots Ritter.

They embrace briefly a moment later and then Ritter motions to the center attraction of the evening.

"That him?" he asks Migs.

"Shit, Ritt, this kid is unbelievable! I never seen nothing like him even when we were chasing rogue brujas through the Andes with the WET team. He's been down here a month and I've watched him eat and drink shit that would turn a harpy inside out. It's like he has some natural immunity to curses and hexes. And the metabolism of a billy goat on meth on top of that."

Ritter just nods, although inwardly he feels a sudden rush of adrenaline, the kind that occurs at the end of a quest.

"Just the boy I've been looking for," Ritter comments casually.

In the middle of the room the master of ceremonies unsheathes a machete and cleanly severs the organ atop the table in half. He sweeps one piece directly in front of Moon and the other in front of the curandera.

The entire bar abruptly goes silent.

All eyes are on the table.

Moon, humming a tune that sounds vaguely like a Green Day song, picks up his knife and fork and cuts into the meat as if it were a grass-fed, medium-rare porterhouse.

He's on his fifth bite by the time the curandera slices one tiny, carefully considered bite and forks it resolutely into her mouth.

She immediately spits it onto the floor, grasping her throat.

A few seconds later her flesh has turned green.

Half the crowd cheers while the other half jeers.

Money is exchanged and tickets are torn apart and cast to the floor.

Moon continues eating happily.

Hours later the bar is empty and the fat MC is getting thoroughly plastered with Migs and his new bartender companion.

Moon is in a corner booth counting the evening's take in half a dozen forms of currency.

Ritter slides into the booth across from him.

He's only carrying one form of currency.

Dollars.

Ten thousand of them.

Which he plops in a bundle atop the table.

"What's this?" Moon asks.

"A signing bonus," Ritter explains. "I want to hire you to come to New York and taste test a bunch of weird magical shit for me on a regular basis."

Moon reaches out and picks up the bundle.

"Like, a regular job?" he asks.

Ritter nods. "Trust me," he says. "For you it's the opportunity of a lifetime."

NOW

It's like no battle Ritter or Cindy has experienced.

They've both been soldiers, but never living war machines, and that's what they are now. The gnome and leprechaun leaders are each directing them to combat the thickest throngs of both sides, decimating front lines on the ground with kicks of their feet.

Cindy is tasked with beating back the Gnomi construct of balled-up armored warriors with her tomahawk, keeping it at bay so it can't break through the leprechaun's multicolored pathways being shot through the air.

Ritter, meanwhile, has been given a short sword with which he severs those same beams as if cutting through a jungle thicket, dissolving them and causing the leprechauns surging across the strips of light to tumble to the ground.

The cavern is streaked with rainbows, over and between and around which spherical armored gnomes are flying every which way. The air is filled with tiny spears, and Ritter is punting leprechauns while trying not to step on any.

Cindy, meanwhile, is using the flat of her tomahawk's blade to bat away gnome balls coming at her from every angle.

Moon watches his teammates from behind a stalagmite. Thus far he's gone unnoticed by both sides.

It's all relatively chill, he thinks, until a gnome flies out of nowhere and banks the side of his skull.

In the next moment Moon is reflexively chewing grit, the crunch more than the mossy taste causing him to spit the dirt from his mouth.

He blinks away blood and sees Ritter besieged by leprechauns, dozens of them scrambling up both of his legs.

Moon turns his head just in time to watch a gnome collide with Cindy's gut and knock the wind from her.

For the first time in a long time Moon—who is insufferable in his nihilism on most days—feels genuinely pissed off.

A warrior of the Tuath Dé leaps into his field of vision, a spear in his hand and a battle cry on his lips.

Moon doesn't even think.

He reaches out, grasps the leprechaun in his fist, and

stuffs the entire being into his mouth.

Fortunately the tiny god drops his spear.

The worst part isn't the chewing.

The leprechaun's screams echo in the chamber of Moon's skull.

That's the worst part.

When he swallows it's agonizing and Moon can feel his mouth and throat being shredded by tiny bones and it is all he can do not to vomit immediately.

Just when he thinks he can't choke it back any longer the urge goes away.

What replaces it is far worse.

Fae magic fills him like a virus, and his body rejects the unnatural energy. It would certainly rip most humans apart rather than be expelled, but Moon was born different for reasons none can guess or discern.

He vomits magical waste from every pore.

And every stream is a projectile.

It sweeps across the cavern floor in waves of blue fire, toppling every gnome and leprechaun in its path. It even sweeps Ritter and Cindy off their feet.

And it just keeps coming.

Moon rises to his knees, screaming as the magic continues to vent from his pores.

The next thing of which he's truly conscious is Ritter tackling him to the ground.

"Stop!" Ritter is begging him, and the raw emotion in his voice, so uncustomary for Ritter, is enough to break Moon's consciousness free of the rapture.

"Moon! Please, stop!"

Appealing to his conscious mind seems to have an energetic effect on the rest of him.

Slowly, he's able to force his body under a shaking, fragile form of control.

The remaining fae magic is reduced to a trickle.

Groaning, his face sticky with sweat and tears, Moon stares blearily from underneath Ritter at the desolation he's created.

The entire cavern floor is littered with tiny bodies.

They all seem even smaller now.

It's like staring across a mass grave, though many are still alive, moaning in their semiconscious state.

What happens next shocks Ritter more than his own pleading startled Moon.

Beneath him, Moon begins to sob.

Ritter cradles him like a child, stroking his damp hair and whispering comforting words in his ear.

Moon clings to his arms, unbidden, tears pouring from him as fiercely as the magic did.

Several yards away what's left of the Gnomi force scrapes across the stony ground, drawing to a center point and slowly forming an even more grotesque, bastardized version of their battle construct, this one missing key portions throughout its form.

The construct limps towards the spot where the few dozen conscious leprechauns are attempting to regroup and attend to their wounded.

Ritter opens his mouth to protest, but in the end he doesn't have to speak a word.

Hara bursts through the armored form like a star running back shredding the opposing team's banner before a game.

Unfurled bodies of armored gnomes are scattered everywhere, most of them knocked unconscious by the force of Hara's dense, almost inhuman mass.

Hara, a true giant among his people, stands there, ever the stoic, surveying the damage without expression.

Ryland staggers around him from behind, looking at Ritter.

"Oh," he says, as if he's just popped in for high tea. "There you are then."

Cindy limps over to where Ritter is cradling Moon, her breath ragged, her torso bleeding in dozens of places and gnomish blood dripping from her tomahawk.

"I think we can go now," she says.

Ritter looks up at her, still holding Moon in his arms. He nods. "What about the gold?"

"I know where we can find as much as we need," she

informs him.

Then, looking over the littered leprechaun bodies: "I don't think they'd mind even if they could stop us at this point. It's no good to them anymore."

"We all end up that way," Ritter says. "Eventually."

Then: "Let's finish the mission."

"Aye-aye," Cindy affirms.

———

Back in their rented Transit, driving away from the abandoned mine filled with its two forgotten, waning worlds, none of them speak for a long time.

The cargo vehicle is weighted down heavily and moves like a sluggish drunk running from his bar tab, but it will get them there.

Them, and all of the gold pressing the back end of the van inches from the road underneath it.

They're silently worried about Moon, who seems to be the worst for their shared experience (except for Ryland, who, even if he fully grasped what had happened while they were separated, probably wouldn't appreciate it).

Moon sits, almost catatonic, for an hour.

Then, abruptly and with deep gravitas, he says: "It sucks being small."

They all look back at him, even Ryland, who has spent just enough time with Moon to know he's not the sort of person who speaks introspectively.

Moon doesn't seem to notice the gazes he's drawn.

He's very much in his own head at that moment.

"I've been small my whole life. It really sucks, you know? And you figure out pretty quick it's useless fighting about being small and about how fuckers treat you when you're small. No one cares. But you still want to fight. So you fight about stupid shit. You'll fight about anything, really. When really you're just fighting because it's better than being shit on and taking it. But it's always about being small. Always."

There are no immediate replies or comments or reassurances offered.

Cindy stares openly at him, completely taken aback.

Ritter keeps his eyes on the road, but the truth of those words, and the illustration of them to which they've all just born witness, digs at the back of his brain.

Ryland lights his thirty-fourth cigarette of the trip.

In the end it's Hara who breaks the wake of oppressive silence.

"It's not easy being big either," he says in a voice that always sounds to Ritter like everyone imagines their father sounds when they're young.

Hara pauses before adding: "But it's a lot easier than

being small."

The rest of them seem to wait for Moon to decide the fate of that statement.

Eventually he laughs, just a little.

"Yeah," he says. "It is."

They all leave it at that.

Acknowledgments

First props always go to Lee Harris, Sin du Jour's editor, who continually teaches me things I should've learned in the writing class I did not attend. The luminous Irene Gallo, Mordicai Knode, Carl Engle-Laird, and the entire staff of Tor.com Publishing, all of whom would be my choice to crew a rogue steampunk pirate airship I was captaining. Alan Tafoya, two-time world knife-fighting champion and master thespian, helped me write authentic Native characters instead of another generation of crude stereotypes. Mur Lafferty, my longtime friend and cohost on the *Ditch Diggers* podcast, who is never not looking to help me do more and better. My agent, Dong-Won Song, who accepted a flaming halberd and agreed to take up the charge. I also have a couple of makeup acknowledgments that rightfully should've been in the first Sin du Jour book. Peter Lutjen, cover designer, who did absolutely nothing I ever envisioned and created the perfect cover because of it. I also want to thank Liana Krissoff, my copyeditor, whom I had not yet met (and technically still haven't) when I composed the acknowledgements for the first book (authors, always thank your copyeditor).

About the Author

Author photograph by Earl Newton

Matt Wallace is the author of *The Next Fix, The Failed Cities,* and his other novella series, Slingers. He's also penned more than one hundred short stories, a few of which have won awards and been nominated for others, in addition to writing for film and television. In his youth he traveled the world as a professional wrestler and un-armed combat and self-defense instructor before retiring to write full time.

He now resides in Los Angeles with the love of his life and inspiration for Sin du Jour's resident pastry chef.

TOR·COM

Science fiction. Fantasy. The universe. And related subjects.

✳

More than just a publisher's website, *Tor.com* is a venue for **original fiction, comics,** and **discussion** of the entire field of SF and fantasy, in all media and from all sources. Visit our site today — and join the conversation yourself.

4797

CPSIA information can be obtained at www.ICGtesting.com
Printed in the USA
LVOW11s0916090316

478410LV00002B/6/P